Marx Hardy Joyce Abbott Machiavelli Chesterton Cooper Emerson Austen Defoe Melville Montaigne Haggard Hugo Grimm Eliot Stoker Carroll Christie Maupassant Byron Molière Wilde Garnett Einstein Fitzgerald Engels Schiller Goethe Hawthorne Smith Kafka Cotton Kipling Doyle Hall Baum Henry Dostoyevsky Willis Leslie Dumas Flaubert Nietzsche Stockton Turgenev Balzac Burroughs Vatsyayana Crane Curtis Tocqueville Verne Homer Widger Tolstoy Gogol Vinci Darwin Thoreau Whitman Busch Potter Freud Zola Lawrence Twain Scott Plato Kant Jowett Stevenson Dickens Harte Andersen Burton Hesse London Descartes Cervantes Poe Aristotle Wells Voltaire Hale James Hastings Cooke Bunner Shakespeare Irving Richter Chambers Doré Dante Chekhov Shaw Benedict Alcott Swift Pushkin Wodehouse Newton

# The Minstrel, or the Progress of Genius with some other poems

James Beattie

# Imprint


This book is part of TREDITION CLASSICS


Author: James Beattie
Cover design: Buchgut, Berlin – Germany

Publisher: tredition GmbH, Hamburg - Germany
ISBN: 978-3-8472-1523-3

www.tredition.com
www.tredition.de


Copyright:
The content of this book is sourced from the public domain.

The intention of the TREDITION CLASSICS series is to make world literature in the public domain available in printed format. Literary enthusiasts and organizations, such as Project Gutenberg, world-wide have scanned and digitally edited the original texts. tredition has subsequently formatted and redesigned the content into a modern reading layout. Therefore, we cannot guarantee the exact reproduction of the original format of a particular historic edition. Please also note that no modifications have been made to the spelling, therefore it may differ from the orthography used today.

# THE
## MINSTREL,
# WITH
## SOME OTHER POEMS.

THE

# MINSTREL;

OR,

# THE PROGRESS OF GENIUS.

WITH

# SOME OTHER POEMS.

By JAMES BEATTIE, LL. D.

## EDINBURGH:

PRINTED BY JAMES BALLANTYNE,
FOR WILLIAM CREECH, MANNERS AND MILLER,
AND A. CONSTABLE AND CO.

### 1805.

TO
SIR WILLIAM FORBES,
OF PITSLIGO, BARONET,

AS A MARK OF RESPECT FOR HIS CHARACTER,
AND AS AN APPROPRIATE TRIBUTE TO ONE OF
THE MOST
VALUED FRIENDS OF THE AUTHOR,

THIS EDITION
OF THE
POETICAL WORKS OF DR BEATTIE,
*IS INSCRIBED*
BY
THE PUBLISHERS.

# PREFACE [ix]
# TO
# THE MINSTREL.

The design was, to trace the progress of a Poetical Genius, born in a rude age, from the first dawning of fancy and reason, till that period at which he may be supposed capable of appearing in the world as a Minstrel, that is, as an itinerant Poet and Musician;—a character, which, according to the notions of our fore-fathers, was not only respectable, but sacred. [x]

I have endeavoured to imitate Spenser in the measure of his verse, and in the harmony, simplicity, and variety, of his composition. Antique expressions I have avoided; admitting, however, some old words, where they seemed to suit the subject; but I hope none will be found that are now obsolete, or in any degree unintelligible to a reader of English poetry.

To those, who may be disposed to ask, what could induce me to write in so difficult a measure, I can only answer, that it pleases my ear, and seems, from its Gothic structure and original, to bear some relation to the subject and spirit of the Poem. It admits both of simplicity and magnificence of sound and of language, beyond any other stanza that I am acquainted with. It allows [xi] the sententiousness of the couplet, as well as the more complex modulation of blank verse. What some critics have remarked, of its uniformity growing at last tiresome to the ear, will be found to hold true, only when the poetry is faulty in other respects.

[1] # THE

## MINSTREL;

# IN TWO BOOKS.

[2]

*Me vero primum dulces ante omnia Musæ,*
*Quarum sacra fero, ingenti perculsus amore,*
*Accipiant. – –*

Virgil.

# THE [3]

# MINSTREL;

# OR,

# THE PROGRESS OF GENIUS.

**BOOK FIRST.**

I.

Ah! who can tell how hard it is to climb
The steep, where Fame's proud temple shines afar!
Ah! who can tell how many a soul sublime
Has felt the influence of malignant star,
And waged with Fortune an eternal war!
Checked by the scoff of Pride, by Envy's frown,
And Poverty's unconquerable bar,
In life's low vale remote has pined alone,
Then dropt into the grave, unpitied and unknown!

II. [4]

And yet, the languor of inglorious days
Not equally oppressive is to all.
Him, who ne'er listened to the voice of praise,
The silence of neglect can ne'er appal.
There are, who, deaf to mad Ambition's call,
Would shrink to hear th' obstreperous trump of Fame;
Supremely blest, if to their portion fall
Health, competence, and peace. Nor higher aim
Had He, whose simple tale these artless lines proclaim.

III.

This sapient age disclaims all classic lore;
Else I should here, in cunning phrase, display,
How forth The Minstrel fared in days of yore,
Right glad of heart, though homely in array;
His waving locks and beard all hoary grey:
And, from his bending shoulder, decent hung
His harp, the sole companion of his way,
Which to the whistling wind responsive rung:
And ever as he went some merry lay he sung.


IV. [5]

Fret not yourselves, ye silken sons of pride,
That a poor Wanderer should inspire my strain.
The Muses fortune's fickle smile deride,
Nor ever bow the knee in Mammon's fane;
For their delights are with the village-train,
Whom Nature's laws engage, and Nature's charms:
They hate the sensual, and scorn the vain;
The parasite their influence never warms,
Nor him whose sordid soul the love of wealth alarms.


V.

Though richest hues the peacock's plumes adorn,
Yet horror screams from his discordant throat.
Rise, sons of harmony, and hail the morn,
While warbling larks on russet pinions float;
Or seek, at noon, the woodland scene remote,
Where the grey linnets carol from the hill.
O let them ne'er, with artificial note,
To please a tyrant, strain the little bill!
But sing what heaven inspires, and wander where they will.

VI. [6]

> Liberal, not lavish, is kind Nature's hand;
> Nor was perfection made for man below.
> Yet all her schemes with nicest art are planned,
> Good counteracting ill, and gladness woe.
> With gold and gems if Chilian mountains glow,
> If bleak and barren Scotia's hills arise;
> There, plague and poison, lust and rapine grow;
> Here, peaceful are the vales, and pure the skies,
> And freedom fires the soul, and sparkles in the eyes.

VII.

> Then grieve not, thou, to whom the indulgent Muse
> Vouchsafes a portion of celestial fire;
> Nor blame the partial fates, if they refuse
> The imperial banquet, and the rich attire.
> Know thine own worth, and reverence the lyre.
> Wilt thou debase the heart which God refined?
> No; let thy heaven-taught soul to heaven aspire,
> To fancy, freedom, harmony, resigned;
> Ambition's grovelling crew for ever left behind.

VIII. [7]

> Canst thou forego the pure ethereal soul
> In each fine sense so exquisitely keen,
> On the dull couch of Luxury to loll,
> Stung with disease, and stupified with spleen;
> Fain to implore the aid of Flattery's screen,
> Even from thyself thy loathsome heart to hide,
> (The mansion, then, no more of joy serene)
> Where fear, distrust, malevolence, abide,
> And impotent desire, and disappointed pride?

IX.

> O, how canst thou renounce the boundless store
> Of charms which Nature to her votary yields!
> The warbling woodland, the resounding shore,
> The pomp of groves, and garniture of fields;
> All that the genial ray of morning gilds,
> And all that echoes to the song of even,
> All that the mountain's sheltering bosom shields,
> And all the dread magnificence of heaven,
> O how canst thou renounce, and hope to be forgiven!

X. [8]

> These charms shall work thy soul's eternal health,
> And love, and gentleness, and joy, impart.
> But these thou must renounce, if lust of wealth
> E'er win its way to thy corrupted heart;
> For ah! it poisons like a scorpion's dart;
> Prompting the ungenerous wish, the selfish scheme,
> The stern resolve, unmoved by pity's smart,
> The troublous day, and long distressful dream.
> Return, my roving Muse! resume thy purposed theme.

XI.

> There lived, in Gothic days, as legends tell,
> A shepherd-swain, a man of low degree;
> Whose sires, perchance, in Fairyland might dwell,
> Sicilian groves, or vales of Arcady;
> But he, I ween, was of the North Countrie:
> A nation famed for song, and beauty's charms;
> Zealous, yet modest; innocent, though free;
> Patient of toil; serene amidst alarms;
> Inflexible in faith; invincible in arms.

XII. [9]

> The shepherd-swain, of whom I mention made,
> On Scotia's mountains fed his little flock;
> The sickle, scythe, or plough, he never swayed;
> An honest heart was almost all his stock;
> His drink the living water from the rock:
> The milky dams supplied his board, and lent
> Their kindly fleece to baffle winter's shock;
> And he, though oft with dust and sweat besprent,
> Did guide and guard their wanderings, wheresoe'er they went.

XIII.

> From labour health, from health contentment springs.
> Contentment opes the source of every joy.
> He envied not, he never thought of kings;
> Nor from those appetites sustained annoy,
> Which chance may frustrate, or indulgence cloy:
> Nor fate his calm and humble hopes beguiled;
> He mourned no recreant friend, nor mistress coy,
> For on his vows the blameless Phœbe smiled,
> And her alone he loved, and loved her from a child.

XIV. [10]

> No jealousy their dawn of love o'ercast,
> Nor blasted were their wedded days with strife;
> Each season looked delightful, as it past,
> To the fond husband, and the faithful wife.
> Beyond the lowly vale of shepherd life
> They never roamed; secure beneath the storm
> Which in Ambition's lofty land is rife,
> Where peace and love are cankered by the worm

Of pride, each bud of joy industrious to deform.


XV.

The wight, whose tale these artless lines unfold,
Was all the offspring of this simple pair.
His birth no oracle or seer foretold:
No prodigy appeared in earth or air,
Nor aught that might a strange event declare.
You guess each circumstance of Edwin's birth;
The parent's transport, and the parent's care;
The gossip's prayer for wealth, and wit, and worth;
And one long summer-day of indolence and mirth.


XVI. [11]

And yet poor Edwin was no vulgar boy;
Deep thought oft seemed to fix his infant eye.
Dainties he heeded not, nor gaude, nor toy,
Save one short pipe of rudest minstrelsy.
Silent when glad; affectionate, though shy;
And now his look was most demurely sad,
And now he laughed aloud, yet none knew why.
The neighbours stared and sighed, yet blessed the lad:
Some deemed him wondrous wise, and some believed him
mad.


XVII.

But why should I his childish feats display?
Concourse, and noise, and toil, he ever fled;
Nor cared to mingle in the clamorous fray
Of squabbling imps; but to the forest sped,
Or roamed at large the lonely mountain's head;

Or, where the maze of some bewildered stream
To deep untrodden groves his footsteps led,
There would he wander wild, 'till Phœbus' beam,
Shot from the western cliff, released the weary team.


XVIII. [12]

The exploit of strength, dexterity, or speed,
To him nor vanity nor joy could bring.
His heart, from cruel sport estranged, would bleed
To work the woe of any living thing,
By trap, or net; by arrow, or by sling;
These he detested, those he scorned to wield:
He wished to be the guardian, not the king,
Tyrant, far less, or traitor, of the field.
And sure the sylvan reign unbloody joy might yield.


XIX.

Lo! where the stripling, wrapt in wonder, roves
Beneath the precipice o'erhung with pine;
And sees, on high, amidst the encircling groves,
From cliff to cliff the foaming torrents shine:
While waters, woods, and winds, in concert join,
And Echo swells the chorus to the skies.
Would Edwin this majestic scene resign
For aught the huntsman's puny craft supplies?
Ah! no: he better knows great Nature's charms to prize.


XX. [13]

And oft he traced the uplands, to survey,
When o'er the sky advanced the kindling dawn,
The crimson cloud, blue main, and mountain grey,

And lake, dim-gleaming on the smoky lawn;
Far to the west the long, long vale withdrawn,
Where twilight loves to linger for a while;
And now he faintly kens the bounding fawn,
And villager abroad at early toil.
But, lo! the sun appears! and heaven, earth, ocean, smile.


XXI.

And oft the craggy cliff he loved to climb,
When all in mist the world below was lost.
What dreadful pleasure! there to stand sublime,
Like shipwrecked mariner on desert coast,
And view the enormous waste of vapour, tost
In billows, lengthening to the horizon round,
Now scooped in gulfs, with mountains now embossed!
And hear the voice of mirth and song rebound,
Flocks, herds, and waterfalls, along the hoar profound!


XXII. [14]

In truth he was a strange and wayward wight,
Fond of each gentle, and each dreadful scene.
In darkness, and in storm, he found delight:
Nor less, than when on ocean-wave serene
The southern sun diffused his dazzling shene.
Even sad vicissitude amused his soul:
And if a sigh would sometimes intervene,
And down his cheek a tear of pity roll,
A sigh, a tear, so sweet, he wished not to controul.


XXIII.

'O ye wild groves, O where is now your bloom!'
(The Muse interprets thus his tender thought.)
'Your flowers, your verdure, and your balmy gloom,
'Of late so grateful in the hour of drought!
'Why do the birds, that song and rapture brought
'To all your bowers, their mansions now forsake?
'Ah! why has fickle chance this ruin wrought!
'For now the storm howls mournful through the brake,
'And the dead foliage flies in many a shapeless flake.


XXIV. [15]

'Where now the rill, melodious, pure, and cool,
'And meads, with life, and mirth, and beauty, crowned!
'Ah! see, the unsightly slime, and sluggish pool,
'Have all the solitary vale imbrowned;
'Fled each fair form, and mute each melting sound.
'The raven croaks forlorn on naked spray:
'And, hark! the river, bursting every mound,
'Down the vale thunders; and, with wasteful sway,
'Uproots the grove, and rolls the shattered rocks away.


XXV.

'Yet such the destiny of all on earth:
'So flourishes and fades majestic man.
'Fair is the bud his vernal morn brings forth,
'And fostering gales awhile the nursling fan.
'O smile, ye heavens, serene; ye mildews wan,
'Ye blighting whirlwinds, spare his balmy prime,
'Nor lessen of his life the little span.
'Borne on the swift, though silent, wings of Time,
'Old-age comes on apace to ravage all the clime.

XXVI. [16]

'And be it so. Let those deplore their doom,
'Whose hope still grovels in this dark sojourn.
'But lofty souls, who look beyond the tomb,
'Can smile at Fate, and wonder how they mourn.
'Shall spring to these sad scenes no more return?
'Is yonder wave the sun's eternal bed?
'Soon shall the orient with new lustre burn,
'And spring shall soon her vital influence shed,
'Again attune the grove, again adorn the mead.

XXVII.

'Shall I be left abandoned in the dust,
'When Fate, relenting, lets the flower revive?
'Shall Nature's voice, to man alone unjust,
'Bid him, though doomed to perish, hope to live?
'Is it for this fair Virtue oft must strive
'With disappointment, penury, and pain?
'No: Heaven's immortal spring shall yet arrive;
'And man's majestic beauty bloom again,
'Bright through the eternal year of Love's triumphant reign.'

XXVIII. [17]

This truth sublime his simple sire had taught.
In sooth, 'twas almost all the shepherd knew.
No subtle nor superfluous lore he sought,
Nor ever wished his Edwin to pursue.
'Let man's own sphere (quoth he) confine his view,
'Be man's peculiar work his sole delight.'
And much, and oft, he warned him, to eschew
Falsehood and guile, and aye maintain the right,
By pleasure unseduced, unawed by lawless might.

XXIX.

'And, from the prayer of Want, and plaint of Woe,
'O never, never turn away thine ear.
'Forlorn, in this bleak wilderness below,
'Ah! what were man, should Heaven refuse to hear!
'To others do (the law is not severe)
'What to thyself thou wishest to be done.
'Forgive thy foes; and love thy parents dear,
'And friends, and native land; nor those alone;
'All human weal and woe learn thou to make thine own.'


XXX. [18]

See, in the rear of the warm sunny shower,
The visionary boy from shelter fly!
For now the storm of summer-rain is o'er,
And cool, and fresh, and fragrant is the sky.
And, lo! in the dark east, expanded high,
The rainbow brightens to the setting sun!
Fond fool, that deem'st the streaming glory nigh,
How vain the chace thine ardour has begun!
'Tis fled afar, ere half thy purposed race be run.


XXXI.

Yet couldst thou learn, that thus it fares with age,
When pleasure, wealth, or power, the bosom warm,
This baffled hope might tame thy manhood's rage,
And Disappointment of her sting disarm. − −
But why should foresight thy fond heart alarm?
Perish the lore that deadens young desire!
Pursue, poor imp, the imaginary charm,
Indulge gay hope, and fancy's pleasing fire:
Fancy and Hope too soon shall of themselves expire.

XXXII. [19]

> When the long-sounding curfew, from afar,
> Loaded with loud lament the lonely gale,
> Young Edwin, lighted by the evening star,
> Lingering and listening, wandered down the vale.
> There would he dream of graves, and corses pale;
> And ghosts, that to the charnel-dungeon throng,
> And drag a length of clanking chain, and wail,
> Till silenced by the owl's terrific song,
> Or blast that shrieks by fits the shuddering aisles along.

XXXIII.

> Or, when the setting moon, in crimson dyed,
> Hung o'er the dark and melancholy deep,
> To haunted stream, remote from man, he hied,
> Where fays, of yore, their revels wont to keep;
> And there let Fancy roam at large, till sleep
> A vision brought to his entranced sight.
> And first, a wildly murmuring wind 'gan creep
> Shrill to his ringing ear; then tapers bright,
> With instantaneous gleam, illumed the vault of night.

XXXIV. [20]

> Anon in view a portal's blazoned arch
> Arose; the trumpet bids the valves unfold;
> And forth an host of little warriors march,
> Grasping the diamond lance, and targe of gold.
> Their look was gentle, their demeanour bold,
> And green their helms, and green their silk attire;
> And here and there, right venerably old,
> The long-robed minstrels wake the warbling wire,
> And some with mellow breath the martial pipe inspire.

XXXV.

> With merriment, and song, and timbrels clear,
> A troop of dames from myrtle bowers advance;
> The little warriors doff the targe and spear,
> And loud enlivening strains provoke the dance.
> They meet, they dart away, they wheel askance;
> To right, to left, they thrid the flying maze;
> Now bound aloft with vigorous spring, then glance
> Rapid along: with many-coloured rays
> Of tapers, gems, and gold, the echoing forests blaze.


XXXVI. [21]

> The dream is fled. Proud harbinger of day,
> Who scar'dst the vision with thy clarion shrill,
> Fell chanticleer! who oft hast reft away
> My fancied good, and brought substantial ill!
> O to thy cursed scream, discordant still,
> Let Harmony aye shut her gentle ear:
> Thy boastful mirth let jealous rivals spill,
> Insult thy crest, and glossy pinions tear,
> And ever in thy dreams the ruthless fox appear.


XXXVII.

> Forbear, my Muse. Let love attune thy line.
> Revoke the spell. Thine Edwin frets not so.
> For how should he at wicked chance repine,
> Who feels, from every change, amusement flow?
> Even now his eyes with smiles of rapture glow,
> As on he wanders through the scenes of morn,
> Where the fresh flowers in living lustre blow,
> Where thousand pearls the dewy lawns adorn,
> A thousand notes of joy in every breeze are borne.

XXXVIII. [22]

But who the melodies of morn can tell?
The wild brook babbling down the mountain side;
The lowing herd; the sheepfold's simple bell;
The pipe of early shepherd, dim descried
In the lone valley; echoing far and wide,
The clamorous horn, along the cliffs above;
The hollow murmur of the ocean-tide;
The hum of bees, and linnet's lay of love,
And the full choir that wakes the universal grove.


XXXIX.

The cottage-curs at early pilgrim bark;
Crowned with her pail the tripping milkmaid sings;
The whistling ploughman stalks afield; and, hark!
Down the rough slope the ponderous waggon rings;
Through rustling corn the hare astonished springs;
Slow tolls the village-clock the drowsy hour;
The partridge bursts away on whirring wings;
Deep mourns the turtle in sequestered bower,
And shrill lark carols clear from her aërial tour.


XL. [23]

O Nature, how in every charm supreme!
Whose votaries feast on raptures ever new!
O for the voice and fire of seraphim,
To sing thy glories with devotion due!
Blessed be the day I 'scaped the wrangling crew,
From Pyrrho's maze, and Epicurus' sty;
And held high converse with the godlike few,
Who to the enraptured heart, and ear, and eye,
Teach beauty, virtue, truth, and love, and melody.

XLI.

> Hence! ye, who snare and stupify the mind,
> Sophists, of beauty, virtue, joy, the bane!
> Greedy and fell, though impotent and blind,
> Who spread your filthy nets in Truth's fair fane,
> And ever ply your venomed fangs amain!
> Hence to dark Error's den, whose rankling slime
> First gave you form! hence! lest the Muse should deign,
> (Though loath on theme so mean to waste a rhyme),
> With vengeance to pursue your sacrilegious crime.


XLII. [24]

> But hail, ye mighty masters of the lay,
> Nature's true sons, the friends of man and truth!
> Whose song, sublimely sweet, serenely gay,
> Amused my childhood, and informed my youth.
> O let your spirit still my bosom sooth,
> Inspire my dreams, and my wild wanderings guide!
> Your voice each rugged path of life can smooth;
> For well I know, wherever ye reside,
> There harmony, and peace, and innocence, abide.


XLIII.

> Ah me! abandoned on the lonesome plain,
> As yet poor Edwin never knew your lore,
> Save when against the winter's drenching rain,
> And driving snow, the cottage shut the door.
> Then, as instructed by tradition hoar,
> Her legends when the Beldam 'gan impart,
> Or chant the old heroic ditty o'er,
> Wonder and joy ran thrilling to his heart;
> Much he the tale admired, but more the tuneful art.

XLIV. [25]

> Various and strange was the long-winded tale;
> And halls, and knights, and feats of arms, displayed;
> Or merry swains, who quaff the nut-brown ale,
> And sing, enamoured of the nut-brown maid;
> The moon-light revel of the fairy glade;
> Or hags, that suckle an infernal brood,
> And ply in caves the unutterable trade,
> 'Midst fiends and spectres, quench the moon in blood,
> Yell in the midnight storm, or ride the infuriate flood.

XLV.

> But when to horror his amazement rose,
> A gentler strain the Beldam would rehearse,
> A tale of rural life, a tale of woes,
> The orphan-babes, and guardian uncle fierce.
> O cruel! will no pang of pity pierce
> That heart by lust of lucre seared to stone!
> For sure, if aught of virtue last, or verse,
> To latest times shall tender souls bemoan
> Those helpless orphan-babes by thy fell arts undone.

XLVI. [26]

> Behold, with berries smeared, with brambles torn,
> The babes, now famished, lay them down to die;
> 'Midst the wild howl of darksome woods forlorn,
> Folded in one another's arms they lie;
> Nor friend, nor stranger, hears their dying cry:
> 'For from the town the man returns no more.'
> But thou, who Heaven's just vengeance darest defy,
> This deed with fruitless tears shalt soon deplore,
> When Death lays waste thy house, and flames consume thy

store.


XLVII.

A stifled smile of stern vindictive joy
Brightened one moment Edwin's starting tear. —
'But why should gold man's feeble mind decoy,
'And innocence thus die by doom severe?'
O Edwin! while thy heart is yet sincere,
The assaults of discontent and doubt repel:
Dark even at noontide is our mortal sphere;
But let us hope; to doubt, is to rebel;
Let us exult in hope, that all shall yet be well.


XLVIII. [27]

Nor be thy generous indignation checked,
Nor checked the tender tear to misery given;
From Guilt's contagious power shall that protect,
This soften and refine the soul for heaven.
But dreadful is their doom, whom doubt hath driven
To censure Fate, and pious hope forego;
Like yonder blasted boughs by lightning riven,
Perfection, beauty, life, they never know,
But frown on all that pass, a monument of woe.


XLIX.

Shall he, whose birth, maturity, and age,
Scarce fill the circle of one summer-day,
Shall the poor gnat, with discontent and rage,
Exclaim that Nature hastens to decay,
If but a cloud obstruct the solar ray,
If but a momentary shower descend!

Or shall frail man Heaven's dread decree gainsay,
Which bade the series of events extend
Wide through unnumbered worlds, and ages without end!


L. [28]

One part, one little part, we dimly scan,
Through the dark medium of life's feverish dream;
Yet dare arraign the whole stupendous plan,
If but that little part incongruous seem.
Nor is that part, perhaps, what mortals deem;
Oft from apparent ill our blessings rise.
O then, renounce that impious self-esteem,
That aims to trace the secrets of the skies:
For thou art but of dust; be humble, and be wise.


LI.

Thus, Heaven enlarged his soul in riper years.
For Nature gave him strength, and fire, to soar,
On Fancy's wing above this vale of tears;
Where dark cold-hearted sceptics, creeping, pore
Through microscope of metaphysic lore:
And much they grope for truth, but never hit.
For why? their powers, inadequate before,
This art preposterous renders more unfit;
Yet deem they darkness light, and their vain blunders wit.


LII. [29]

Nor was this ancient dame a foe to mirth.
Her ballad, jest, and riddle's quaint device,
Oft cheered the shepherds round their social hearth;
Whom levity or spleen could ne'er entice

To purchase chat or laughter at the price
Of decency. Nor let it faith exceed,
That Nature forms a rustic taste so nice.
Ah! had they been of court or city breed,
Such delicacy were right marvellous indeed.


LIII.

Oft when the winter-storm had ceased to rave,
He roamed the snowy waste at even, to view
The cloud stupendous, from the Atlantic wave
High-towering, sail along the horizon blue:
Where, 'midst the changeful scenery ever new,
Fancy a thousand wondrous forms descries,
More wildly great than ever pencil drew;
Rocks, torrents, gulfs, and shapes of giant size,
And glittering cliffs on cliffs, and fiery ramparts rise.


LIV. [30]

Thence, musing, onward to the sounding shore,
The lone enthusiast oft would take his way,
Listening, with pleasing dread, to the deep roar
Of the wide-weltering waves. In black array
When sulphurous clouds rolled on the vernal day,
Even then he hastened from the haunt of man,
Along the darkening wilderness to stray,
What time the lightning's fierce career began,
And o'er heaven's rending arch the rattling thunder ran.


LV.

Responsive to the sprightly pipe, when all
In sprightly dance the village-youth were joined,

Edwin, of melody aye held in thrall,
From the rude gambol far remote reclined,
Soothed with the soft notes warbling in the wind.
Ah then, all jollity seemed noise and folly.
To the pure soul, by Fancy's fire refined,
Ah, what is mirth, but turbulence unholy,
When with the charm compared of heavenly melancholy!


LVI. [31]

Is there a heart that music cannot melt?
Ah me! how is that rugged heart forlorn!
Is there, who ne'er those mystic transports felt,
Of solitude and melancholy born?
He needs not woo the Muse; he is her scorn.
The sophist's rope of cobweb he shall twine;
Mope o'er the schoolman's peevish page; or mourn,
And delve for life, in Mammon's dirty mine;
Sneak with the scoundrel fox, or grunt with glutton swine.


LVII.

For Edwin, Fate a nobler doom had planned;
Song was his favourite and first pursuit.
The wild harp rang to his adventurous hand,
And languished to his breath the plaintive flute.
His infant muse, though artless, was not mute:
Of elegance, as yet, he took no care;
For this of time and culture is the fruit;
And Edwin gained, at last, this fruit so rare:
As in some future verse I purpose to declare.


LVIII. [32]

Meanwhile, whate'er of beautiful, or new,
Sublime, or dreadful, in earth, sea, or sky,
By chance, or search, was offered to his view,
He scanned with curious and romantic eye.
Whate'er of lore tradition could supply
From Gothic tale, or song, or fable old,
Roused him, still keen to listen and to pry.
At last, though long by penury controuled,
And solitude, his soul her graces 'gan unfold.


LIX.

Thus, on the chill Lapponian's dreary land,
For many a long month lost in snow profound,
When Sol from Cancer sends the season bland,
And in their northern cave the storms hath bound;
From silent mountains, straight, with startling sound,
Torrents are hurled; green hills emerge; and lo,
The trees with foliage, cliffs with flowers are crowned;
Pure rills through vales of verdure warbling go;
And wonder, love, and joy, the peasant's heart o'erflow.


LX. [33]

Here pause, my Gothic lyre, a little while.
The leisure hour is all that thou can'st claim.
But on this verse if Montagu should smile,
New strains, ere long, shall animate thy frame:
And his applause to me is more than fame;
For still with truth accords his taste refined.
At lucre or renown let others aim,
I only wish to please the gentle mind,
Whom Nature's charms inspire, and love of humankind.
[34]

# [35] THE

# MINSTREL;

# BOOK SECOND.

*Doctrina sed vim promovet insitam,*
*Rectique cultus pectora roborant.*

Horat. [36]

# THE [37]

# MINSTREL;

# OR,

# THE PROGRESS OF GENIUS.

**BOOK SECOND.**

I.

Of chance or change, O let not man complain,
Else shall he never never cease to wail:
For, from the imperial dome, to where the swain
Rears the lone cottage in the silent dale,
All feel the assault of fortune's fickle gale;
Art, empire, earth itself, to change are doomed;
Earthquakes have raised to heaven the humble vale;
And gulfs the mountain's mighty mass entombed;
And where the Atlantic rolls wide continents have bloomed.


II. [38]

But sure to foreign climes we need not range,
Nor search the ancient records of our race,
To learn the dire effects of time and change,
Which in ourselves, alas! we daily trace.
Yet, at the darkened eye, the withered face,
Or hoary hair, I never will repine:
But spare, O Time, whate'er of mental grace,
Of candour, love, or sympathy divine,
Whate'er of fancy's ray, or friendship's flame, is mine.

III.

> So I, obsequious to Truth's dread command,
> Shall here, without reluctance, change my lay,
> And smite the Gothic lyre with harsher hand;
> Now when I leave that flowery path, for aye,
> Of childhood, where I sported many a day,
> Warbling, and sauntering carelessly along;
> Where every face was innocent and gay,
> Each vale romantic, tuneful every tongue,
> Sweet, wild, and artless all, as Edwin's infant song.

IV. [39]

> 'Perish the lore that deadens young desire,'
> Is the soft tenor of my song no more.
> Edwin, though loved of heaven, must not aspire
> To bliss, which mortals never knew before.
> On trembling wings let youthful fancy soar,
> Nor always haunt the sunny realms of joy,
> But now and then the shades of life explore;
> Though many a sound and sight of woe annoy,
> And many a qualm of care his rising hopes destroy.

V.

> Vigour from toil, from trouble patience grows.
> The weakly blossom, warm in summer bower,
> Some tints of transient beauty may disclose;
> But ah, it withers in the chilling hour.
> Mark yonder oaks! Superior to the power
> Of all the warring winds of heaven, they rise,
> And from the stormy promontory tower,
> And toss their giant arms amid the skies,
> While each assailing blast increase of strength supplies.

VI. [40]

> And now the downy cheek and deepened voice
> Gave dignity to Edwin's blooming prime;
> And walks of wider circuit were his choice,
> And vales more wild, and mountains more sublime.
> One evening, as he framed the careless rhyme,
> It was his chance to wander far abroad,
> And o'er a lonely eminence to climb,
> Which heretofore his foot had never trode;
> A vale appeared below, a deep retired abode.

VII.

> Thither he hied, enamoured of the scene:
> For rocks on rocks piled, as by magic spell,
> Here scorched with lightning, there with ivy green,
> Fenced from the north and east this savage dell;
> Southward a mountain rose with easy swell,
> Whose long long groves eternal murmur made;
> And toward the western sun a streamlet fell,
> Where, through the cliffs, the eye, remote, surveyed
> Blue hills, and glittering waves, and skies in gold arrayed.

VIII. [41]

> Along this narrow valley, you might see
> The wild deer sporting on the meadow ground,
> And, here and there, a solitary tree,
> Or mossy stone, or rock with woodbine crowned.
> Oft did the cliffs reverberate the sound
> Of parted fragments tumbling from on high;
> And, from the summit of that craggy mound,
> The perching eagle oft was heard to cry,
> Or on resounding wings to shoot athwart the sky.

IX.

One cultivated spot there was, that spread
Its flowery bosom to the noon-day beam,
Where many a rose-bud rears its blushing head,
And herbs, for food, with future plenty teem.
Soothed by the lulling sound of grove and stream,
Romantic visions swarm on Edwin's soul:
He minded not the sun's last trembling gleam,
Nor heard from far the twilight curfew toll,
When slowly on his ear these moving accents stole.


X. [42]

'Hail, awful scenes, that calm the troubled breast,
'And woo the weary to profound repose;
'Can passion's wildest uproar lay to rest,
'And whisper comfort to the man of woes!
'Here Innocence may wander, safe from foes,
'And Contemplation soar on seraph wings.
'O Solitude, the man who thee foregoes,
'When lucre lures him, or ambition stings,
'Shall never know the source whence real grandeur springs.


XI.

'Vain man, is grandeur given to gay attire?
'Then let the butterfly thy pride upbraid:
'To friends, attendants, armies, bought with hire?
'It is thy weakness that requires their aid:
'To palaces, with gold and gems inlaid?
'They fear the thief, and tremble in the storm:
'To hosts, through carnage who to conquest wade?
'Behold the victor vanquished by the worm!
'Behold what deeds of woe the locust can perform!

XII. [43]

'True dignity is his, whose tranquil mind
'Virtue has raised above the things below;
'Who, every hope and fear to heaven resigned,
'Shrinks not, though Fortune aim her deadliest blow.'
This strain, from midst the rocks, was heard to flow
In solemn sounds. Now beamed the evening-star;
And from embattled clouds, emerging slow,
Cynthia came riding on her silver car;
And hoary mountain-cliffs shone faintly from afar.


XIII.

Soon did the solemn voice its theme renew;
(While Edwin, wrapt in wonder, listening stood)
'Ye tools and toys of tyranny, adieu;
'Scorned by the wise, and hated by the good!
'Ye only can engage the servile brood
'Of Levity and Lust, who, all their days,
'Ashamed of truth and liberty, have wooed,
'And hugged the chain, that, glittering on their gaze,
'Seems to outshine the pomp of heaven's empyreal blaze.


XIV. [44]

'Like them, abandoned to Ambition's sway,
'I sought for glory in the paths of guile;
'And fawned and smiled, to plunder and betray,
'Myself betrayed and plundered all the while;
'So gnawed the viper the corroding file.
'But now, with pangs of keen remorse, I rue
'Those years of trouble and debasement vile.
'Yet why should I this cruel theme pursue?
'Fly, fly, detested thoughts, for ever from my view!

XV.

'The gusts of appetite, the clouds of care,
'And storms of disappointment, all o'erpast,
'Henceforth, no earthly hope with heaven shall share
'This heart, where peace serenely shines at last.
'And if for me no treasure be amassed,
'And if no future age shall hear my name,
'I lurk the more secure from fortune's blast,
'And with more leisure feed this pious flame,
'Whose rapture far transcends the fairest hopes of fame.


XVI. [45]

'The end and the reward of toil is rest.
'Be all my prayer for virtue and for peace.
'Of wealth and fame, of pomp and power possessed,
'Who ever felt his weight of woe decrease!
'Ah! what avails the lore of Rome and Greece,
'The lay, heaven-prompted, and harmonious string,
'The dust of Ophir, or the Tyrian fleece,
'All that art, fortune, enterprise, can bring,
'If envy, scorn, remorse, or pride, the bosom wring!


XVII.

'Let Vanity adorn the marble tomb
'With trophies, rhymes, and scutcheons of renown,
'In the deep dungeon of some Gothic dome,
'Where night and desolation ever frown.
'Mine be the breezy hill that skirts the down;
'Where a green grassy turf is all I crave,
'With here and there a violet bestrown,
'Fast by a brook, or fountain's murmuring wave;
'And many an evening sun shine sweetly on my grave.

XVIII. [46]

'And thither let the village swain repair;
'And, light of heart, the village maiden gay,
'To deck with flowers her half-dishevelled hair,
'And celebrate the merry morn of May.
'There let the shepherd's pipe, the live-long day,
'Fill all the grove with love's bewitching woe;
'And when mild Evening comes with mantle grey,
'Let not the blooming band make haste to go;
'No ghost, nor spell, my long and last abode shall know.


XIX.

'For though I fly to 'scape from fortune's rage,
'And bear the scars of envy, spite, and scorn,
'Yet with mankind no horrid war I wage,
'Yet with no impious spleen my breast is torn:
'For virtue lost, and ruined man, I mourn.
'O Man! creation's pride, heaven's darling child,
'Whom Nature's best, divinest, gifts adorn,
'Why from thy home are truth and joy exiled,
'And all thy favourite haunts with blood and tears defiled!


XX. [47]

'Along yon glittering sky what glory streams!
'What majesty attends night's lovely queen!
'Fair laugh our vallies in the vernal beams;
'And mountains rise, and oceans roll between,
'And all conspire to beautify the scene.
'But, in the mental world, what chaos drear!
'What forms of mournful, loathsome, furious mien!
'O when shall that eternal morn appear,
'These dreadful forms to chace, this chaos dark to clear!

XXI.

> 'O Thou, at whose creative smile, yon heaven,
> 'In all the pomp of beauty, life, and light,
> 'Rose from the abyss; when dark Confusion, driven
> 'Down down the bottomless profound of night,
> 'Fled, where he ever flies thy piercing sight!
> 'O glance on these sad shades one pitying ray,
> 'To blast the fury of oppressive might,
> 'Melt the hard heart to love and mercy's sway,
> 'And cheer the wandering soul, and light him on the way.'


XXII. [48]

> Silence ensued: and Edwin raised his eyes
> In tears, for grief lay heavy at his heart.
> 'And is it thus in courtly life,' (he cries)
> 'That man to man acts a betrayer's part?
> 'And dares he thus the gifts of heaven pervert,
> 'Each social instinct, and sublime desire?
> 'Hail Poverty! if honour, wealth, and art,
> 'If what the great pursue, and learned admire,
> 'Thus dissipate and quench the soul's ethereal fire!'


XXIII.

> He said, and turned away; nor did the Sage
> O'erhear, in silent orisons employed.
> The Youth, his rising sorrow to assuage,
> Home as he hied, the evening scene enjoyed:
> For now no cloud obscures the starry void;
> The yellow moonlight sleeps on all the hills;
> Nor is the mind with startling sounds annoyed;
> A soothing murmur the lone region fills,
> Of groves, and dying gales, and melancholy rills.

XXIV. [49]

But he, from day to day, more anxious grew.
The voice still seemed to vibrate on his ear.
Nor durst he hope the Hermit's tale untrue;
For man he seemed to love, and heaven to fear;
And none speaks false, where there is none to hear.
'Yet, can man's gentle heart become so fell?
'No more in vain conjecture let me wear
'My hours away, but seek the Hermit's cell;
'Tis he my doubt can clear, perhaps my care dispel.'


XXV.

At early dawn the youth his journey took,
And many a mountain passed, and valley wide,
Then reached the wild; where, in a flowery nook,
And seated on a mossy stone, he spied
An ancient man: his harp lay him beside.
A stag sprang from the pasture at his call,
And, kneeling, licked the withered hand, that tied
A wreath of woodbine round his antlers tall,
And hung his lofty neck with many a floweret small.


XXVI. [50]

And now the hoary Sage arose, and saw
The wanderer approaching: innocence
Smiled on his glowing cheek, but modest awe
Depressed his eye, that feared to give offence.
'Who art thou, courteous stranger? and from whence?
'Why roam thy steps to this abandoned dale?'
'A shepherd-boy (the Youth replied), far hence
'My habitation; hear my artless tale;
'Nor levity nor falsehood shall thine ear assail.

XXVII.

    'Late as I roamed, intent on Nature's charms,
    'I reached, at eve, this wilderness profound;
    'And, leaning where yon oak expands her arms,
    'Heard these rude cliffs thine awful voice rebound,
    '(For, in thy speech, I recognise the sound.)
    'You mourned for ruined man, and virtue lost,
    'And seemed to feel of keen remorse the wound,
    'Pondering on former days, by guilt engrossed,
    'Or in the giddy storm of dissipation tossed.


XXVIII. [51]

    'But say, in courtly life can craft be learned,
    'Where knowledge opens, and exalts the soul?
    'Where Fortune lavishes her gifts unearned,
    'Can selfishness the liberal heart controul?
    'Is glory there achieved by arts, as foul
    'As those which felons, fiends, and furies plan?
    'Spiders ensnare, snakes poison, tygers prowl;
    'Love is the godlike attribute of man.
    'O teach a simple Youth this mystery to scan!


XXIX.

    'Or else the lamentable strain disclaim,
    'And give me back the calm, contented mind;
    'Which, late, exulting, viewed, in Nature's frame,
    'Goodness untainted, wisdom unconfined,
    'Grace, grandeur, and utility combined.
    'Restore those tranquil days, that saw me still
    'Well pleased with all, but most with humankind;
    'When Fancy roamed through Nature's works at will,
    'Unchecked by cold distrust, and uninformed of ill.'

XXX. [52]

    'Wouldst thou (the Sage replied) in peace return
    'To the gay dreams of fond romantic youth,
    'Leave me to hide, in this remote sojourn,
    'From every gentle ear the dreadful truth:
    'For if my desultory strain with ruth
    'And indignation make thine eyes o'erflow,
    'Alas! what comfort could thy anguish sooth,
    'Shouldst thou the extent of human folly know?
    'Be ignorance thy choice, where knowledge leads to woe.


XXXI.

    'But let untender thoughts afar be driven;
    'Nor venture to arraign the dread decree:
    'For know, to man, as candidate for heaven,
    'The voice of The Eternal said, Be free:
    'And this divine prerogative to thee
    'Does virtue, happiness, and heaven convey;
    'For virtue is the child of liberty,
    'And happiness of virtue; nor can they
    'Be free to keep the path, who are not free to stray.


XXXII. [53]

    'Yet leave me not. I would allay that grief,
    'Which else might thy young virtue overpower;
    'And in thy converse I shall find relief,
    'When the dark shades of melancholy lower:
    'For solitude has many a dreary hour,
    'Even when exempt from grief, remorse, and pain:
    'Come often then; for, haply, in my bower,
    'Amusement, knowledge, wisdom, thou may'st gain:
    'If I one soul improve, I have not lived in vain.'

XXXIII.

    And now, at length, to Edwin's ardent gaze
    The Muse of History unrolls her page.
    But few, alas! the scenes her art displays,
    To charm his fancy, or his heart engage.
    Here, chiefs their thirst of power in blood assuage,
    And straight their flames with tenfold fierceness burn:
    Here, smiling Virtue prompts the patriot's rage,
    But lo, ere long, is left alone to mourn,
    And languish in the dust, and clasp the abandoned urn.


XXXIV. [54]

    'Ah, what avails (he said) to trace the springs
    'That whirl of empire the stupendous wheel!
    'Ah, what have I to do with conquering kings,
    'Hands drenched in blood, and breasts begirt with steel!
    'To those, whom Nature taught to think and feel,
    'Heroes, alas! are things of small concern.
    'Could History man's secret heart reveal,
    'And what imports a heaven-born mind to learn,
    'Her transcripts to explore what bosom would not yearn!


XXXV.

    'This praise, O Cheronean Sage, is thine.
    '(Why should this praise to thee alone belong!)
    'All else from Nature's moral path decline,
    'Lured by the toys that captivate the throng;
    'To herd in cabinets and camps, among
    'Spoil, carnage, and the cruel pomp of pride;
    'Or chaunt of heraldry the drowsy song,
    'How tyrant blood, o'er many a region wide,
    'Rolls to a thousand thrones its execrable tide.

XXXVI. [55]

'O, who of man the story will unfold,
'Ere victory and empire wrought annoy,
'In that elysian age (misnamed of gold)
'The age of love, and innocence, and joy,
'When all were great and free! man's sole employ
'To deck the bosom of his parent earth;
'Or toward his bower the murmuring stream decoy,
'To aid the floweret's long-expected birth,
'And lull the bed of peace, and crown the board of mirth.


XXXVII.

'Sweet were your shades, O ye primeval groves,
'Whose boughs to man his food and shelter lent,
'Pure in his pleasures, happy in his loves,
'His eye still smiling, and his heart content.
'Then, hand in hand, Health, Sport, and Labour went.
'Nature supplied the wish she taught to crave.
'None prowled for prey, none watched to circumvent.
'To all an equal lot Heaven's bounty gave:
'No vassal feared his lord, no tyrant feared his slave.


XXXVIII. [56]

'But ah! the Historic Muse has never dared
'To pierce those hallowed bowers: 'tis Fancy's beam,
'Poured on the vision of the enraptured Bard,
'That paints the charms of that delicious theme.
'Then hail sweet Fancy's ray! and hail the dream
'That weans the weary soul from guilt and woe!
'Careless what others of my choice may deem,
'I long where Love and Fancy lead to go,
'And meditate on heaven; enough of earth I know.'

XXXIX.

     'I cannot blame thy choice (the Sage replied),
     'For soft and smooth are Fancy's flowery ways.
     'And yet, even there, if left without a guide,
     'The young adventurer unsafely plays.
     'Eyes, dazzled long by Fiction's gaudy rays,
     'In modest Truth no light nor beauty find.
     'And who, my child, would trust the meteor-blaze,
     'That soon must fail, and leave the wanderer blind,
     'More dark and helpless far, than if it ne'er had shined?

XL. [57]

     'Fancy enervates, while it sooths, the heart,
     'And, while it dazzles, wounds the mental sight:
     'To joy each heightening charm it can impart,
     'But wraps the hour of woe in tenfold night.
     'And often, where no real ills affright,
     'Its visionary fiends, an endless train,
     'Assail with equal or superior might,
     'And through the throbbing heart, and dizzy brain,
     'And shivering nerves, shoot stings of more than mortal pain.

XLI.

     'And yet, alas! the real ills of life
     'Claim the full vigour of a mind prepared;
     'Prepared for patient, long, laborious strife,
     'Its guide Experience, and Truth its guard.
     'We fare on earth, as other men have fared:
     'Were they successful? Let not us despair.
     'Was disappointment oft their sole reward?
     'Yet shall their tale instruct, if it declare,
     'How they have borne the load ourselves are doomed to

bear.


XLII. [58]

   'What charms the Historic Muse adorn, from spoils,
'And blood, and tyrants, when she wings her flight,
'To hail the patriot Prince, whose pious toils
'Sacred to science, liberty, and right,
'And peace, through every age divinely bright,
'Shall shine the boast and wonder of mankind!
'Sees yonder sun, from his meridian height,
'A lovelier scene, than Virtue thus inshrined
'In power, and man with man for mutual aid combine!


XLIII.

   'Hail, sacred Polity, by Freedom reared!
'Hail, sacred Freedom, when by Law restrained!
'Without you what were man? A grovelling herd,
'In darkness, wretchedness, and want enchained.
'Sublimed by you, the Greek and Roman reigned
'In arts unrivalled: O, to latest days,
'In Albion may your influence, unprofaned,
'To godlike worth the generous bosom raise,
'And prompt the Sage's lore, and fire the Poet's lays.


XLIV. [59]

   'But now let other themes our care engage.
'For lo, with modest, yet majestic grace,
'To curb Imagination's lawless rage,
'And from within the cherished heart to brace,
'Philosophy appears. The gloomy race,
'By Indolence and moping Fancy bred,

'Fear, Discontent, Solicitude give place,
'And Hope and Courage brighten in their stead,
'While on the kindling soul her vital beams are shed.


XLV.

'Then waken from long lethargy to life
'The seeds of happiness, and powers of thought;
'Then jarring appetites forego their strife,
'A strife by ignorance to madness wrought.
'Pleasure by savage man is dearly bought
'With fell revenge, lust that defies controul,
'With gluttony and death. The mind untaught,
'Is a dark waste, where fiends and tempests howl;
'As Phœbus to the world, is Science to the soul.


XLVI. [60]

'And Reason, now, through Number, Time, and Space,
'Darts the keen lustre of her serious eye,
'And learns, from facts compared, the laws to trace,
'Whose long progression leads to Deity.
'Can mortal strength presume to soar so high?
'Can mortal sight, so oft bedimmed with tears,
'Such glory bear? — for lo, the shadows fly
'From Nature's face; Confusion disappears,
'And order charms the eyes, and harmony the ears.


XLVII.

'In the deep windings of the grove, no more
'The hag obscene, and grisly phantom dwell;
'Nor in the fall of mountain-stream, or roar
'Of winds, is heard the angry spirit's yell;

'No wizard mutters the tremendous spell,
'Nor sinks convulsive in prophetic swoon;
'Nor bids the noise of drums and trumpets swell,
'To ease of fancied pangs the labouring moon,
'Or chace the shade that blots the blazing orb of noon.


XLVIII. [61]

'Many a long lingering year, in lonely isle,
'Stunned with the eternal turbulence of waves,
'Lo, with dim eyes, that never learned to smile,
'And trembling hands, the famished native craves
'Of Heaven his wretched fare: shivering in caves,
'Or scorched on rocks, he pines from day to day;
'But Science gives the word; and lo, he braves
'The surge and tempest, lighted by her ray,
'And to a happier land wafts merrily away.


XLIX.

'And even where Nature loads the teeming plain
'With the full pomp of vegetable store,
'Her bounty, unimproved, is deadly bane:
'Dark woods and rankling wilds, from shore to shore,
'Stretch their enormous gloom; which, to explore,
'Even Fancy trembles, in her sprightliest mood;
'For there, each eyeball gleams with lust of gore,
'Nestles each murderous and each monstrous brood,
'Plague lurks in every shade, and streams from every flood.


L. [62]

''Twas from Philosophy man learned to tame
'The soil, by plenty to intemperance fed.

'Lo, from the echoing axe, and thundering flame,
'Poison, and plague, and yelling rage, are fled.
'The waters, bursting from their slimy bed,
'Bring health and melody to every vale:
'And, from the breezy main, and mountain's head,
'Ceres and Flora, to the sunny dale,
'To fan their glowing charms, invite the fluttering gale.

LI.

'What dire necessities, on every hand,
'Our art, our strength, our fortitude, require!
'Of foes intestine, what a numerous band
'Against this little throb of life conspire!
'Yet Science can elude their fatal ire
'Awhile, and turn aside Death's levelled dart,
'Sooth the sharp pang, allay the fever's fire,
'And brace the nerves once more, and cheer the heart,
'And yet a few soft nights and balmy days impart.

LII. [63]

'Nor less to regulate man's moral frame
'Science exerts her all-composing sway.
'Flutters thy breast with fear, or pants for fame,
'Or pines, to indolence and spleen a prey,
'Or avarice, a fiend more fierce than they?
'Flee to the shade of Academus' grove;
'Where cares molest not, discord melts away
'In harmony, and the pure passions prove,
'How sweet the words of truth, breathed from the lips of
Love.

LIII.

'What cannot Art and Industry perform,
'When Science plans the progress of their toil!
'They smile at penury, disease, and storm;
'And oceans from their mighty mounds recoil.
'When tyrants scourge, or demagogues embroil
'A land, or when the rabble's headlong rage
'Order transforms to anarchy and spoil,
'Deep-versed in man, the philosophic Sage
'Prepares, with lenient hand, their phrenzy to assuage.


LIV. [64]

''Tis he alone, whose comprehensive mind,
'From situation, temper, soil, and clime
'Explored, a nation's various powers can bind,
'And various orders, in one form sublime
'Of polity, that, midst the wrecks of time,
'Secure shall lift its head on high, nor fear
'The assault of foreign or domestic crime,
'While public Faith, and public Love sincere,
'And Industry and Law maintain their sway severe.'


LV.

Enraptured by the Hermit's strain, the Youth
Proceeds the path of science to explore.
And now, expanding to the beams of truth,
New energies, and charms unknown before,
His mind discloses: Fancy now no more
Wantons on fickle pinion through the skies;
But, fixed in aim, and conscious of her power,
Sublime from cause to cause exults to rise,
Creation's blended stores arranging as she flies.

LVI. [65]

> Nor love of novelty alone inspires,
> Their laws and nice dependencies to scan;
> For, mindful of the aids that life requires,
> And of the services man owes to man,
> He meditates new arts on Nature's plan;
> The cold desponding breast of Sloth to warm,
> The flame of Industry and Genius fan,
> And Emulation's noble rage alarm,
> And the long hours of Toil and Solitude to charm.

LVII.

> But She, who set on fire his infant heart,
> And all his dreams, and all his wanderings shared
> And blessed, the Muse, and her celestial art,
> Still claim the Enthusiast's fond and first regard.
> From Nature's beauties variously compared,
> And variously combined, he learns to frame
> Those forms of bright perfection, which the Bard,
> While boundless hopes and boundless views inflame,
> Enamoured consecrates to never-dying fame.

LVIII. [66]

> Of late, with cumbersome, though pompous show,
> Edwin would oft his flowery rhyme deface,
> Through ardour to adorn; but Nature now
> To his experienced eye a modest grace
> Presents, where Ornament the second place
> Holds, to intrinsic worth and just design
> Subservient still. Simplicity apace
> Tempers his rage: he owns her charm divine,
> And clears the ambiguous phrase, and lops the unwieldy

line.


LIX.

Fain would I sing (much yet unsung remains)
What sweet delirium o'er his bosom stole,
When the great Shepherd of the Mantuan plains
His deep majestic melody 'gan roll:
Fain would I sing, what transport stormed his soul,
How the red current throbbed his veins along,
When, like Pelides, bold beyond controul,
Gracefully terrible, sublimely strong,
Homer raised high to heaven the loud, the impetuous song.


LX. [67]

And how his lyre, though rude her first essays,
Now skilled to sooth, to triumph, to complain,
Warbling at will through each harmonious maze,
Was taught to modulate the artful strain,
I fain would sing: but ah! I strive in vain.
Sighs from a breaking heart my voice confound.
With trembling step, to join yon weeping train,
I haste, where gleams funereal glare around,
And, mixed with shrieks of woe, the knells of death resound.


LXI.

Adieu, ye lays, that fancy's flowers adorn,
The soft amusement of the vacant mind!
He sleeps in dust, and all the Muses mourn,
He, whom each virtue fired, each grace refined,
Friend, teacher, pattern, darling of mankind!
He sleeps in dust. Ah! how should I pursue

My theme! To heart-consuming grief resigned,
Here, on his recent grave I fix my view,
And pour my bitter tears. — Ye flowery lays, adieu!


LXII. [68]

Art thou, my Gregory, for ever fled!
And am I left to unavailing woe!
When fortune's storms assail this weary head,
Where cares long since have shed untimely snow,
Ah, now for comfort whither shall I go!
[69] No more thy soothing voice my anguish chears:
Thy placid eyes with smiles no longer glow,
My hopes to cherish, and allay my fears.
[70] 'Tis meet that I should mourn: — flow forth afresh my
tears.

**[71] POEMS**

**ON**

# SEVERAL OCCASIONS.

**RETIREMENT.**
**1758.**

When, in the crimson cloud of Even,
The lingering light decays,
And Hesper, on the front of heaven,
His glittering gem displays;
Deep in the silent vale, unseen,
Beside a lulling stream,
A pensive Youth, of placid mien,
Indulged this tender theme. [72]


Ye cliffs, in hoary grandeur piled,
High o'er the glimmering dale;
Ye woods, along whose windings wild,
Murmurs the solemn gale;
Where Melancholy strays forlorn,
And Woe retires to weep,
What time the wan moon's yellow horn
Gleams on the western deep.


To you, ye wastes, whose artless charms
Ne'er drew Ambition's eye,
'Scaped a tumultuous world's alarms,
To your retreats I fly.
Deep in your most sequestered bower,
Let me at last recline,

Where Solitude, mild, modest power,
Leans on her ivy'd shrine.


How shall I woo thee, matchless Fair!
Thy heavenly smile how win! [73]
Thy smile, that smooths the brow of care,
And stills the storm within.
O wilt thou to thy favourite grove
Thine ardent votary bring,
And bless his hours, and bid them move,
Serene, on silent wing.


Oft let remembrance sooth his mind
With dreams of former days,
When, in the lap of peace reclined,
He framed his infant lays;
When Fancy roved at large, nor Care,
Nor cold Distrust alarmed,
Nor Envy, with malignant glare,
His simple youth had harmed.


'Twas then, O Solitude, to thee
His early vows were paid,
From heart sincere, and warm, and free,
Devoted to the shade. [74]
Ah why did Fate his steps decoy
In stormy paths to roam,
Remote from all congenial joy? —
O take the Wanderer home!


Thy shades, thy silence, now be mine,
Thy charms my only theme;
My haunt the hollow cliff, whose pine
Waves o'er the gloomy stream,
Whence the scared owl, on pinions grey,

Breaks from the rustling boughs,
And down the lone vale sails away
To more profound repose.


O! while to thee the woodland pours
Its wildly warbling song,
And balmy from the bank of flowers
The zephyr breathes along;
Let no rude sound invade from far,
No vagrant foot be nigh, [75]
No ray from Grandeur's gilded car,
Flash on the startled eye.


But if some pilgrim through the glade,
Thy hallowed bowers explore,
O guard from harm his hoary head,
And listen to his lore;
For he of joys divine shall tell,
That wean from earthly woe,
And triumph o'er the mighty spell,
That chains this heart below.


For me, no more the path invites
Ambition loves to tread;
No more I climb those toilsome heights
By guileful Hope misled;
Leaps my fond fluttering heart no more
To Mirth's enlivening strain;
For present pleasure soon is o'er,
And all the past is vain.

## ELEGY. [76]

Still shall unthinking man substantial deem
The forms, that fleet through life's deceitful dream?
On clouds, where Fancy's beam amusive plays,
Shall heedless Hope the towering fabric raise?
Till at Death's touch the fairy visions fly,
And real scenes rush dismal on the eye;
And, from Elysium's balmy slumber torn,
The startled soul awakes, to think, and mourn.
O ye, whose hours in jocund train advance,
Whose spirits to the song of gladness dance,
Who flowery vales in endless view survey,
Glittering in beams of visionary day;
O, yet while Fate delays the impending woe,
Be roused to thought, anticipate the blow;
Lest, like the lightning's glance, the sudden ill
Flash to confound, and penetrate to kill; [77]
Lest, thus encompassed with funereal gloom,
Like me, ye bend o'er some untimely tomb,
Pour your wild ravings in Night's frighted ear,
And half pronounce Heaven's sacred doom severe.
Wise, beauteous, good! O every grace combined,
That charms the eye, or captivates the mind!
Fair, as the floweret opening on the morn,
Whose leaves bright drops of liquid pearl adorn!
Sweet, as the downy-pinioned gale, that roves
To gather fragrance in Arabian groves!
Mild, as the strains, that, at the close of day,
Warbling remote, along the vales decay!
Yet, why with these compared? What tints so fine,
What sweetness, mildness, can be matched with thine?
Why roam abroad? Since still, to Fancy's eyes,
I see, I see thy lovely form arise.
Still let me gaze, and every care beguile,
Gaze on that cheek, where all the Graces smile;
That soul-expressing eye, benignly bright,
Where meekness beams ineffable delight; [78]
That brow, where Wisdom sits enthroned serene,

Each feature forms, and dignifies the mein:
Still let me listen, while her words impart
The sweet effusions of the blameless heart,
Till all my soul, each tumult charmed away,
Yields, gently led, to Virtue's easy sway.
By thee inspired, O Virtue! Age is young,
And music warbles from the faltering tongue:
Thy ray creative cheers the clouded brow,
And decks the faded cheek with rosy glow,
Brightens the joyless aspect, and supplies
Pure heavenly lustre to the languid eyes:
But when Youth's living bloom reflects thy beams,
Resistless on the view the glory streams;
Love, Wonder, Joy, alternately alarm,
And Beauty dazzles with angelic charm.
Ah! whither fled! ye dear illusions, stay!
Lo, pale and silent lies the lovely clay!
How are the roses on that cheek decay'd,
Which late the purple light of youth display'd! [79]
Health on her form each sprightly grace bestow'd;
With life and thought each speaking feature glow'd.
Fair was the flower, and soft the vernal sky;
Elate with hope, we deemed no tempest nigh;
When lo! a whirlwind's instantaneous gust
Left all its beauties withering in the dust!
All cold the hand, that soothed Woe's weary head!
And quenched the eye, the pitying tear that shed!
And mute the voice, whose pleasing accents stole,
Infusing balm into the rankled soul!
O Death! why arm with cruelty thy power,
And spare the idle weed, yet lop the flower?
Why fly thy shafts in lawless error driven?
Is Virtue then no more the care of Heaven?
But peace, bold thought! be still my bursting heart!
We, not Eliza, felt the fatal dart.
Scaped the dark dungeon, does the slave complain,
Nor bless the hand that broke the galling chain?
Say, pines not Virtue for the lingering morn,
On this dark wild condemned to roam forlorn? [80]

Where Reason's meteor-rays, with sickly glow,
O'er the dun gloom a dreadful glimmering throw?
Disclosing dubious to the affrighted eye
O'erwhelming mountains tottering from on high,
Black billowy seas in storm perpetual toss'd,
And weary ways in wildering labyrinths lost.
O happy stroke, that bursts the bonds of clay,
Darts through the rending gloom the blaze of day,
And wings the soul with boundless flight to soar,
Where dangers threat, and fear alarms no more!
Transporting thought! here let me wipe away
The tear of grief, and wake a bolder lay.
But ah! the swimming eye o'erflows anew,
Nor check the sacred drops to pity due;
Lo! where in speechless, hopeless anguish, bend
O'er her loved dust, the Parent, Brother, Friend!
How vain the hope of man!—But cease the strain,
Nor Sorrow's dread solemnity profane;
Mixed with yon drooping mourners, on her bier
In silence shed the sympathetic tear.


## ODE TO HOPE. [81]

I. 1.

O thou, who glad'st the pensive soul,
More than Aurora's smile the swain forlorn,
Left all night long to mourn
Where desolation frowns, and tempests howl;
And shrieks of woe, as intermits the storm,
Far o'er the monstrous wilderness resound,
And cross the gloom darts many a shapeless form,
And many a fire-eyed visage glares around,
O come, and be once more my guest!
Come, for thou oft thy suppliant's vow hast heard,
And oft with smiles indulgent cheer'd,

And soothed him into rest.
[82]


I. 2.

Smit by thy rapture-beaming eye,
Deep flashing through the midnight of their mind,
The sable bands combined,
Where Fear's black banner bloats the troubled sky,
Appalled retire. Suspicion hides her head,
Nor dares th' obliquely gleaming eye-ball raise;
Despair, with gorgon-figured veil o'erspread,
Speeds to dark Phlegethon's detested maze.
Lo, startled at the heavenly ray,
With speed unwonted Indolence upsprings,
And, heaving, lifts her leaden wings,
And sullen glides away.


I. 3.

Ten thousand forms, by pining Fancy view'd,
Dissolve. Above the sparkling flood
When Phœbus rears his awful brow,
From lengthening lawn and valley low [83]
The troops of fen-born mists retire.
Along the plain
The joyous swain
Eyes the gay villages again,
And gold-illumined spire;
While, on the billowy ether borne,
Floats the loose lay's jovial measure;
And light along the fairy Pleasure,
Her green robes glittering to the morn,
Wantons on silken wing. And goblins all
To the damp dungeon shrink, or hoary hall,
Or westward, with impetuous flight,

Shoot to the desert realms of their congenial Night.


II. 1.

When first on Childhood's eager gaze
Life's varied landscape, stretch'd immense around,
Starts out of night profound,
Thy voice incites to tempt th' untrodden maze. [84]
Fond he surveys thy mild maternal face,
His bashful eye still kindling as he views,
And, while thy lenient arm supports his pace,
With beating heart the upland path pursues:
The path that leads, where, hung sublime,
And seen afar, youth's gallant trophies, bright
In Fancy's rainbow ray, invite
His wingy nerves to climb.


II. 2.

Pursue thy pleasurable way,
Safe in the guidance of thy heavenly guard,
While melting airs are heard,
And soft-eyed cherub forms around thee play:
Simplicity, in careless flowers array'd,
Prattling amusive in his accent meek;
And Modesty, half turning as afraid,
The smile just dimpling on his glowing cheek; [85]
Content and Leisure, hand in hand
With Innocence and Peace, advance, and sing;
And Mirth, in many a mazy ring,
Frisks o'er the flowery land.


II. 3.

Frail man, how various is thy lot below!
To-day though gales propitious blow,
And Peace, soft gliding down the sky,
Lead Love along and Harmony,
To-morrow the gay scene deforms;
Then all around
The thunder's sound
Rolls rattling on through heaven's profound,
And down rush all the storms.
Ye days, that balmy influence shed,
When sweet Childhood, ever sprightly,
In paths of pleasure sported lightly,
Whither, ah, whither are ye fled! [86]
Ye cherub train, that brought him on his way,
O leave him not midst tumult and dismay;
For now youth's eminence he gains:
But what a weary length of lingering toil remains!


III. 1.

They shrink, they vanish into air.
Now Slander taints with pestilence the gale;
And mingling cries assail,
The wail of Woe, and groans of grim Despair.
Lo, wizard Envy from his serpent eye
Darts quick destruction in each baleful glance;
Pride, smiling stern, and yellow Jealousy,
Frowning Disdain, and hagard Hate advance;
Behold, amidst the dire array,
Pale wither'd Care his giant-stature rears,
And lo, his iron hand prepares
To grasp its feeble prey.
[87]


III. 2.

Who now will guard bewildered youth
Safe from the fierce assaults of hostile rage?
Such war can Virtue wage,
Virtue, that bears the sacred shield of Truth!
Alas! full oft on Guilt's victorious car
The spoils of Virtue are in triumph borne;
While the fair captive, marked with many a scar,
In lone obscurity, oppressed, forlorn,
Resigns to tears her angel form.
Ill-fated youth, then, whither wilt thou fly?
No friend, no shelter now is nigh,
And onward rolls the storm.


III. 3.

But whence the sudden beam that shoots along?
Why shrink aghast the hostile throng?
Lo, from amidst Affliction's night,
Hope bursts, all radiant, on the sight: [88]
Her words the troubled bosom sooth.
"Why thus dismayed?
"Though foes invade,
"Hope ne'er is wanting to their aid,
"Who tread the path of truth.
"'Tis I, who smooth the rugged way,
"I, who close the eyes of Sorrow,
"And with glad visions of to-morrow
"Repair the weary soul's decay.
"When Death's cold touch thrills to the freezing heart,
"Dreams of heaven's opening glories I impart,
"Till the freed spirit springs on high,
"In rapture too severe for weak Mortality."

[89] *PYGMÆO-GERANO-MACHIA,*

# THE BATTLE OF

# THE PIGMIES AND CRANES.

**FROM THE LATIN OF ADDISON.**

The pygmy-people, and the feathered train,
Mingling in mortal combat on the plain,
I sing. Ye Muses, favour my designs,
Lead on my squadrons, and arrange the lines;
The flashing swords and fluttering wings display,
And long bills nibbling in the bloody fray;
Cranes darting with disdain on tiny foes,
Conflicting birds and men, and war's unnumbered woes!
[90]
The wars and woes of heroes six feet long
Have oft resounded in Pierian song.
Who has not heard of Colchos' golden fleece,
And Argo, manned with all the flower of Greece?
Of Thebes' fell brethren, Theseus, stern of face,
And Peleus' son, unrivalled in the race,
Æneas, founder of the Roman line,
And William, glorious on the banks of Boyne?
Who has not learned to weep at Pompey's woes,
And over Blackmore's epic page to doze?
'Tis I, who dare attempt unusual strains,
Of hosts unsung, and unfrequented plains;
The small shrill trump, and chiefs of little size,
And armies rushing down the darkened skies.
Where India reddens to the early dawn,
Winds a deep vale from vulgar eyes withdrawn:
Bosomed in groves the lowly region lies,
And rocky mountains round the border rise.
Here, till the doom of Fate its fall decreed,
The empire flourished of the pygmy-breed; [91]

Here Industry performed, and Genius planned,
And busy multitudes o'erspread the land.
But now to these lone bounds if pilgrim stray,
Tempting through craggy cliffs the desperate way,
He finds the puny mansion fallen to earth,
Its godlings mouldering on th' abandoned hearth;
And starts, where small white bones are spread around,
"Or little footsteps lightly print the ground;"
While the proud crane her nest securely builds,
Chattering amid the desolated fields.
But different fates befel her hostile rage,
While reigned, invincible through many an age,
The dreaded Pygmy: roused by war's alarms,
Forth rushed the madding Mannikin to arms.
Fierce to the field of death the hero flies;
The faint crane, fluttering, flaps the ground, and dies;
And by the victor borne (o'erwhelming load!)
With bloody bill loose-dangling marks the road.
And oft the wily dwarf in ambush lay,
And often made the callow young his prey; [92]
With slaughtered victims heaped his board, and smiled,
To visit the sire's trespass on the child.
Oft, where his feathered foe had reared her nest,
And laid her eggs and household gods to rest,
Burning for blood, in terrible array,
The eighteen-inch militia burst their way:
All went to wreck; the infant foeman fell,
When scarce his chirping bill had broke the shell.
Loud uproar hence, and rage of arms arose,
And the fell rancour of encountering foes;
Hence dwarfs and cranes one general havoc whelms,
And Death's grim visage scares the pygmy realms.
Not half so furious blazed the warlike fire
Of Mice, high theme of the Meonian lyre;
When bold to battle marched the accoutered Frogs,
And the deep tumult thundered through the bogs.
Pierced by the javelin-bulrush on the shore,
Here, agonizing, rolled the mouse in gore;
And there the frog (a scene full sad to see!)

Shorn of one leg, slow sprawled along on three: [93]
He vaults no more with vigorous hops on high,
But mourns in hoarsest croaks his destiny.
And now the day of woe drew on apace,
A day of woe to all the pygmy-race,
When dwarfs were doomed (but penitence was vain)
To rue each broken egg, and chicken slain.
For roused to vengeance by repeated wrong,
From distant climes the long-billed legions throng:
From Strymon's lake, Cayster's plashy meads,
And fens of Scythia green with rustling reeds;
From where the Danube winds through many a land,
And Mareotis laves the Egyptian strand,
To rendezvous they waft on eager wing,
And wait assembled the returning spring.
Meanwhile they trim their plumes for length of flight,
Whet their keen beaks, and twisting claws, for fight;
Each crane the pygmy power in thought o'erturns,
And every bosom for the battle burns.
When genial gales the frozen air unbind,
The screaming legions wheel, and mount the wind. [94]
Far in the sky they form their long array,
And land and ocean stretch'd immense survey, ·
Deep, deep beneath; and triumphing in pride,
With clouds and winds commixed, innumerous ride;
'Tis wild obstreperous clangour all, and heaven
Whirls, in tempestuous undulation driven.
Nor less the alarm that shook the world below,
Where marched in pomp of war the embattled foe;
Where mannikins with haughty step advance,
And grasp the shield, and couch the quivering lance;
To right and left the lengthening lines they form,
And ranked in deep array await the storm.
High in the midst the chieftain-dwarf was seen,
Of giant stature, and imperial mien.
Full twenty inches tall, he strode along,
And viewed with lofty eye the wondering throng;
And, while with many a scar his visage frowned,
Bared his broad bosom, rough with many a wound

Of beaks and claws, disclosing to their sight
The glorious meed of high heroic might. [95]
For with insatiate vengeance, he pursued,
And never-ending hate, the feathery brood.
Unhappy they, confiding in the length
Of horny beak, or talon's crooked strength,
Who durst abide his rage; the blade descends,
And from the panting trunk the pinion rends.
Laid low in dust the pinion waves no more,
The trunk, disfigured, stiffens in its gore.
What hosts of heroes fell beneath his force!
What heaps of chicken-carnage marked his course!
How oft, O Strymon, thy lone banks along,
Did wailing Echo waft the funeral song!
And now from far the mingling clamours rise,
Loud and more loud rebounding through the skies.
From skirt to skirt of heaven, with stormy sway,
A cloud rolls on, and darkens all the day.
Near and more near descends the dreadful shade,
And now in battleous array displayed,
On sounding wings, and screaming in their ire,
The cranes rush onward, and the fight require. [96]
The pygmy warriors eye, with fearless glare,
The host thick swarming o'er the burthened air:
Thick swarming now, but to their native land
Doomed to return a scanty, straggling band. —
When sudden, darting down the depth of heaven,
Fierce on the expecting foe the cranes are driven.
The kindling phrensy every bosom warms,
The region echoes to the crash of arms:
Loose feathers from the encountering armies fly,
And in careering whirlwinds mount the sky.
To breathe from toil upsprings the panting crane,
Then with fresh vigour downward darts again.
Success in equal balance hovering hangs.
Here, on the sharp spear, mad with mortal pangs,
The bird transfixed in bloody vortex whirls,
Yet fierce in death the threatening talon curls;
There, while the life-blood bubbles from his wound,

With little feet the pygmy beats the ground;
Deep from his breast the short, short sob he draws,
And, dying, curses the keen-pointed claws. [97]
Trembles the thundering field, thick covered o'er
With falchions, mangled wings, and streaming gore,
And pygmy arms, and beaks of ample size;
And here a claw, and there a finger lies.
Encompassed round with heaps of slaughtered foes,
All grim in blood the pygmy champion glows;
And on the assailing host impetuous springs,
Careless of nibbling bills, and flapping wings;
And midst the tumult wheresoe'er he turns,
The battle with redoubled fury burns.
From every side the avenging cranes, amain,
Throng, to o'erwhelm this terror of the plain.
When suddenly (for such the will of Jove)
A fowl enormous, sousing from above,
The gallant chieftain clutched, and, soaring high,
(Sad chance of battle!) bore him up the sky.
The cranes pursue, and, clustering in a ring,
Chatter triumphant round the captive king.
But, ah! what pangs each pygmy bosom wrung,
When, now to cranes a prey, on talons hung, [98]
High in the clouds they saw their helpless lord,
His wriggling form still lessening as he soared!
Lo! yet again, with unabated rage,
In mortal strife the mingling hosts engage.
The crane with darted bill assaults the foe,
Hovering; then wheels aloft to scape the blow:
The dwarf in anguish aims the vengeful wound;
But whirls in empty air the falchion round.
Such was the scene, when midst the loud alarms
Sublime the eternal Thunderer rose in arms;
When Briareus, by mad ambition driven,
Heaved Pelion huge, and hurled it high at heaven.
Jove rolled redoubling thunders from on high,
Mountains and bolts encountered in the sky;
Till one stupendous ruin whelmed the crew,
Their vast limbs weltering wide in brimstone blue.

But now at length the pygmy legions yield,
And, winged with terror, fly the fatal field.
They raise a weak and melancholy wail,
All in distraction scattering o'er the vale. [99]
Prone on their routed rear the cranes descend;
Their bills bite furious, and their talons rend:
With unrelenting ire they urge the chace,
Sworn to exterminate the hated race.
'Twas thus the Pygmy Name, once great in war,
For spoils of conquered cranes renown'd afar,
Perished. For, by the dread decree of Heaven,
Short is the date to earthly grandeur given,
And vain are all attempts to roam beyond
Where Fate has fixed the everlasting bound.
Fallen are the trophies of Assyrian power,
And Persia's proud dominion is no more;
Yea, though to both superior far in fame,
Thine empire, Latium! is an empty name.
And now, with lofty chiefs of antient time,
The pygmy heroes roam the Elysian clime.
Or, if belief to matron-tales be due,
Full oft, in the belated shepherd's view,
Their frisking forms, in gentle green arrayed,
Gambol secure along the moonlight glade. [100]
Secure, for no alarming cranes molest,
And all their woes in long oblivion rest;
Down the deep dale, and narrow winding way,
They foot it featly, ranged in ringlets gay:
'Tis joy and frolic all, where'er they rove,
And Fairy-people is the name they love.

# [101] EPISTLE

# TO

## THE HONOURABLE C. B.

PETERHEAD, 1766.

When B* * * invites me, and inviting sings,
Instant I'd fly, (had heaven vouchsafed me wings)
To hail him in that calm sequestered seat,
Whence he looks down with pity on the great;
And, midst the groves retired, at leisure wooes
Domestic love, contentment, and the Muse.
I wish for wings and winds to speed my course;
Since B— —t and the fates refuse a horse.
Where now the Pegasus of antient time,
And Ippogrifo famed in modern rhime? [102]
O, where that wooden steed, whose every leg
Like lightning flew, obsequious to the peg;
The waxen wings by Dædalus designed,
And China waggons wafted by the wind?
A Spaniard reached the moon, upborn by geese;
(Then first 'twas known that she was made of cheese.)
A fidler on a fish through waves advanced,
He twanged his catgut, and the Dolphin danced.
Hags rode on broom-sticks, heathen-gods on clouds;
Ladies, on rams and bulls, have dared the floods.
Much famed the shoes Jack Giant-killer wore,
And Fortunatus' hat is famed much more.
Such vehicles were common once, no doubt;
But modern versemen must even trudge on foot,
Or doze at home, expectants of the gout.
Hard is the task, indeed 'tis wondrous hard,
To act the Hirer, yet preserve the Bard.
"Next week, by — —, (but 'tis a sin to swear)
"I give my word, sir, you shall have my mare; [103]
"Sound wind and limb, as any ever was,

"And rising only seven years old next grass.
"Four miles an hour she goes, nor needs a spur;
"A pretty piece of flesh, upon my conscience, sir."
This speech was B— —t's; and, tho' mean in phrase,
The nearest thing to prose, as Horace says,
(Satire the fourth, and forty-second line)
'Twill intimate that I propose to dine
Next week with B***. Muse, lend thine aid a while;
For this great purpose claims a lofty style.
Ere yonder sun, now glorious in the west,
Has thrice three times reclined on Thetis' breast;
Ere thrice three times, from old Tithonus' bed,
Her charms all glowing with celestial red,
The balmy morn shall rise to mortal view,
And from her bright locks shake the pearls of dew,
These eyes, O B***, shall hail thy opening glades,
These ears shall catch the music of thy shades;
This cherished frame shall drink the gladsome gales,
And the fresh fragrance of thy flowery vales. [104]
And (for I know the Muse will come along)
To B*** I mean to meditate a song:
A song, adorned with every rural charm,
Trim as thy garden, ample as thy farm,
Sweet as thy milk, and brisk as bottled beer,
Wholesome as mutton, and as water clear,
In wildflowers fertile, as thy fields of corn,
And frolicksome as lambs, or sheep new shorn.
I ask not ortolans, or Chian wine,
The fat of rams, or quintessence of swine.
Her spicy stores let either India keep,
Nor El Dorado vend her golden sheep.
And to the mansion house, or council hall,
Still on her black splay feet may the huge tortoise crawl.
Not Parson's butt my appetite can move,
Nor, Bell, thy beer; nor even thy nectar, Jove.
If B*** be happy, and in health, his guest,
Whom wit and learning charm, can wish no better feast.

**[105] THE**

**HARES,**

**A FABLE.**

Yes, yes, I grant the sons of earth
Are doomed to trouble from their birth:
We all of sorrow have our share;
But say, Is your's without compare?
Look round the world; perhaps you'll find
Each individual of our kind
Pressed with an equal load of ill,
Equal at least. Look further still,
And own your lamentable case
Is little short of happiness.
In yonder hut, that stands alone,
Attend to Famine's feeble moan; [106]
Or view the couch where Sickness lies;
Mark his pale cheek, and languid eyes,
His frame by strong convulsion torn,
His struggling sighs, and looks forlorn.
Or see, transfixed with keener pangs,
Where o'er his hoard the miser hangs;
Whistles the wind; he starts, he stares,
Nor Slumber's balmy blessing shares;
Despair, Remorse, and Terror roll
Their tempests on his harassed soul.
But here, perhaps, it may avail
To enforce our reasoning with a tale.
Mild was the morn, the sky serene,
The jolly hunting band convene;
The beagle's breast with ardour burns;
The bounding steed the champaign spurns;
And fancy oft the game descries
Through the hound's nose, and huntsman's eyes.

Just then, a council of the hares
Had met, on national affairs. [107]
The chiefs were set; while o'er their head
The furze its frizzled covering spread.
Long lists of grievances were heard,
And general discontent appeared.
"Our harmless race shall every savage,
"Both quadruped and biped, ravage?
"Shall horses, hounds, and hunters still
"Unite their wits to work us ill?
"The youth, his parent's sole delight,
"Whose tooth the dewy lawns invite,
"Whose pulse in every vein beats strong,
"Whose limbs leap light the vales along,
"May yet e'er noontide meet his death,
"And lie dismembered on the heath:
"For youth, alas! nor cautious age,
"Nor strength, nor speed, eludes their rage.
"In every field we meet the foe,
"Each gale comes fraught with sounds of woe:
"The morning but awakes our fears,
"The evening sees us bathed in tears. [108]
"But must we ever idly grieve,
"Nor strive our fortunes to relieve?
"Small is each individual force,
"To stratagem be our recourse;
"And then, from all our tribes combined,
"The murderer to his cost may find,
"No foe is weak, whom Justice arms,
"Whom Concord leads, and Hatred warms.
"Be roused; or liberty acquire,
"Or in the great attempt expire." —
He said no more, for in his breast
Conflicting thoughts the voice suppressed:
The fire of vengeance seemed to stream
From his swoln eyeball's yellow gleam.
And now the tumults of the war,
Mingling confusedly from afar,
Swell in the wind. Now louder cries,

Distinct, of hounds and men arise.
Forth from the brake, with beating heart,
Th' assembled hares tumultuous start, [109]
And, every straining nerve on wing,
Away precipitately spring.
The hunting band, a signal given,
Thick thundering o'er the plain are driven;
O'er cliff abrupt, and shrubby mound,
And river broad, impetuous bound;
Now plunge amid the forest shades,
Glance through the openings of the glades;
Now o'er the level valley sweep,
Now with short steps strain up the steep,
While backward from the hunter's eyes
The landscape like a torrent flies.
At last an ancient wood they gained,
By pruner's axe yet unprofaned.
High o'er the rest, by Nature reared,
The oak's majestic boughs appeared;
Beneath, a copse of various hue
In barbarous luxuriance grew;
No knife had curbed the rambling sprays,
No hand had wove th' implicit maze. [110]
The flowering thorn, self-taught to wind,
The hazle's stubborn stem intwined,
And bramble twigs were wreathed around,
And rough furze crept along the ground.
Here sheltering, from the sons of murther,
The hares drag their tired limbs no further.
But, lo! the western wind erelong
Was loud, and roared the woods among:
From rustling leaves, and crashing boughs,
The sound of woe and war arose.
The hares, distracted, scour the grove,
As terror and amazement drove;
But danger, wheresoe'er they fled,
Still seemed impending o'er their head.
Now crowded in a grotto's gloom,
All hope extinct, they wait their doom:

Dire was the silence, till, at length,
Even from despair deriving strength,
With bloody eye, and furious look,
A daring youth arose, and spoke. [111]
"O wretched race, the scorn of Fate,
"Whom ills of every sort await!
"O, cursed with keenest sense to feel
"The sharpest sting of every ill!
"Say ye, who, fraught with mighty scheme,
"Of liberty and vengeance dream,
"What now remains? To what recess
"Shall we our weary steps address,
"Since Fate is evermore pursuing
"All ways and means to work our ruin?
"Are we alone, of all beneath,
"Condemned to misery worse than death!
"Must we, with fruitless labour, strive,
"In misery worse than death to live!
"No. Be the smaller ill our choice:
"So dictates Nature's powerful voice.
"Death's pang will in a moment cease;
"And then, All hail, eternal peace!"
Thus while he spoke, his words impart
The dire resolve to every heart. [112]
A distant lake in prospect lay,
That, glittering in the solar ray,
Gleamed through the dusky trees, and shot
A trembling light along the grot.
Thither with one consent they bend,
Their sorrows with their lives to end;
While each, in thought, already hears
The water hissing in his ears,
Fast by the margin of the lake,
Concealed within a thorny brake,
A linnet sate, whose careless lay
Amused the solitary day.
Careless he sung, for on his breast
Sorrow no lasting trace impressed;
When suddenly he heard a sound

Of swift feet traversing the ground.
Quick to the neighbouring tree he flies,
Thence, trembling, casts around his eyes;
No foe appeared, his fears were vain;
Pleased, he renews the sprightly strain. [113]
The hares, whose noise had caused his fright,
Saw, with surprise, the linnet's flight.
Is there on earth a wretch, they said,
Whom our approach can strike with dread?
An instantaneous change of thought
To tumult every bosom wrought.
So fares the system-building sage,
Who, plodding on from youth to age,
At last, on some foundation-dream,
Has reared aloft his goodly scheme,
And proved his predecessors fools,
And bound all nature by his rules;
So fares he, in that dreadful hour,
When injured truth exerts her power,
Some new phenomenon to raise;
Which, bursting on his frighted gaze,
From its proud summit to the ground,
Proves the whole edifice unsound.
"Children," thus spake a hare sedate,
Who oft had known the extremes of Fate, [114]
"In slight events the attentive mind
"May hints of good instruction find.
"That our condition is the worst,
"And we with such misfortunes cursed
"As all comparison defy,
"Was late the universal cry.
"When, lo! an accident so slight,
"As yonder little linnet's flight,
"Has made your stubborn hearts confess
"(So your amazement bids me guess)
"That all our load of woes and fears
"Is but a part of what he bears.
"Where can he rest secure from harms,
"Whom even a helpless hare alarms?

"Yet he repines not at his lot;
"When past, his dangers are forgot:
"On yonder bough he trims his wings,
"And with unusual rapture sings;
"While we, less wretched, sink beneath
"Our lighter ills, and rush to death. [115]
"No more of this unmeaning rage,
"But hear, my friends, the word of age:
"When, by the winds of autumn driven,
"The scattered clouds fly cross the heaven,
"Oft have we, from some mountain's head,
"Beheld the alternate light and shade
"Sweep the long vale. Here, hovering, lowers
"The shadowy cloud; there, downward pours,
"Streaming direct, a flood of day,
"Which from the view flies swift away;
"It flies, while other shades advance,
"And other streaks of sunshine glance.
"Thus chequered is the life below
"With gleams of joy, and clouds of woe.
"Then hope not, while we journey on,
"Still to be basking in the sun;
"Nor fear, though now in shades ye mourn,
"That sunshine will no more return.
"If, by your terrors overcome,
"Ye fly before the approaching gloom, [116]
"The rapid clouds your flight pursue,
"And darkness still o'ercasts your view.
"Who longs to reach the radiant plain,
"Must onward urge his course amain;
"For doubly swift the shadow flies,
"When 'gainst the gale the pilgrim plies.
"At least be firm, and undismayed
"Maintain your ground; the fleeting shade,
"Erelong, spontaneous glides away,
"And gives you back the enlivening ray.
"Lo! while I speak, our danger past!
"No more the shrill horn's angry blast
"Howls in our ear; the savage roar

"Of war and murder is no more.
"Then snatch the hour that Fate allows,
"Nor think of past and future woes."
He spoke; and hope revives; the lake
That instant, one and all forsake,
In sweet amusement to employ
The present sprightly hour of joy. [117]
Now, from the western mountain's brow,
Compassed with clouds of various glow,
The sun a broader orb displays,
And shoots aslope his ruddy rays.
The lawn assumes a fresher green,
And dew-drops spangle all the scene.
The balmy zephyr breathes along,
The shepherd sings his tender song.
With all their lays the groves resound,
And falling waters murmur round;
Discord and care were put to flight,
And all was peace, and calm delight.


## [118] EPITAPH:

## BEING PART OF AN INSCRIPTION FOR A MONUMENT TO BE
## ERECTED BY A GENTLEMAN TO THE MEMORY OF HIS LADY.

Farewell, my best beloved! whose heavenly mind
Genius with virtue, strength with softness, joined;
Devotion, undebased by pride or art,
With meek simplicity, and joy of heart;
Though sprightly, gentle; though polite, sincere;
And only of thyself a judge severe;
Unblamed, unequalled, in each sphere of life,
The tenderest Daughter, Sister, Parent, Wife.
In thee their patroness the afflicted lost;

Thy friends, their pattern, ornament, and boast;
And I— —but, ah! can words my loss declare,
Or paint the extremes of transport and despair?
O Thou, beyond what verse or speech can tell,
My guide, my friend, my best-beloved, farewell!


# [119] ODE

# ON

**LORD HAY'S BIRTH-DAY.**

**13TH MAY, 1767.**

A muse, unskilled in venal praise,
Unstained with flattery's art;
Who loves simplicity of lays
Breathed ardent from the heart;
While gratitude and joy inspire,
Resumes the long-unpractised lyre,
To hail, O Hay, thy natal Morn;
No gaudy wreath of flowers she weaves,
But twines with oak the laurel leaves,
Thy cradle to adorn. [120]
For, not on beds of gaudy flowers
Thine ancestors reclined,
Where sloth dissolves, and spleen devours,
All energy of mind;
To hurl the dart, to ride the car,
To stem the deluges of war,
And snatch from Fate a sinking land;
Trample the invader's lofty crest,
And from his grasp the dagger wrest,
And desolating brand:

'Twas this that raised the illustrious line,
To match the first in fame;
A thousand years have seen it shine
With unabated flame:
Have seen thy mighty sires appear
Foremost in Glory's high career,
The pride and pattern of the brave.
Yet, pure from lust of blood their fire,
And from Ambition's wild desire,
They triumphed but to save. [121]


The Muse with joy attends their way
The vales of peace along;
There, to its Lord the village gay
Renews the grateful song.
Yon castle's glittering towers contain
No pit of woe, nor clanking chain,
Nor to the suppliant's wail resound:
The open doors the needy bless.
The unfriended hail their calm recess,
And gladness smiles around.


There, to the sympathetic heart
Life's best delights belong,
To mitigate the mourner's smart,
To guard the weak from wrong.
Ye sons of luxury, be wise;
Know, happiness for ever flies
The cold and solitary breast;
Then let the social instinct glow,
And learn to feel another's woe,
And in his joy be blessed. [122]

O yet, ere Pleasure plant her snare
For unsuspecting youth;
Ere Flattery her song prepare
To check the voice of Truth;
O may his country's guardian power
Attend the slumbering Infant's bower,
And bright, inspiring dreams impart;
To rouse the hereditary fire,
To kindle each sublime desire,
Exalt, and warm the heart.


Swift to reward a parent's fears,
A parent's hopes to crown,
Roll on in peace, ye blooming years,
That rear him to renown;
When, in his finished form and face,
Admiring multitudes shall trace
Each patrimonial charm combined;
The courteous yet majestic mien,
The liberal smile, the look serene,
The great and gentle mind. [123]


Yet, though thou draw a nation's eyes,
And win a nation's love,
Let not thy towering mind despise
The village and the grove.
No slander there shall wound thy fame,
No ruffian take his deadly aim,
No rival weave the secret snare:
For Innocence, with angel smile,
Simplicity, that knows not guile,
And Love and Peace are there.


When winds the mountain oak assail,
And lay its glories waste,
Content may slumber in the vale,

Unconscious of the blast.
Through scenes of tumult while we roam,
The heart, alas! is ne'er at home;
It hopes in time to roam no more:
The mariner, not vainly brave,
Combats the storm, and rides the wave,
To rest, at last, on shore. [124]


Ye proud, ye selfish, ye severe,
How vain your mask of state!
The good alone have joy sincere,
The good alone are great:
Great, when, amid the vale of peace,
They bid the plaint of sorrow cease,
And hear the voice of artless praise;
As, when along the trophied plain,
Sublime they lead the victor train,
While shouting nations gaze.


# [125] TO

## THE RIGHT HONOURABLE

## LADY CHARLOTTE GORDON,

## DRESSED IN A TARTAN SCOTCH BONNET,

## WITH FEATHERS, &c.


Why, Lady, wilt thou bind thy lovely brow,
With the dread semblance of that warlike helm,
That nodding plume, and wreath of various glow,

That graced the chiefs of Scotia's antient realm?

Thou knowest that virtue is of power the source,
And all her magic to thy eyes is given;
We own their empire, while we feel their force,
Beaming with the benignity of heaven. [126]

The plumy helmet, and the martial mien,
Might dignify Minerva's awful charms;
But more resistless far the Idalian queen—
Smiles, graces, gentleness, her only arms.


# [127] THE
# HERMIT.

At the close of the day, when the hamlet is still,
And mortals the sweets of forgetfulness prove,
When nought but the torrent is heard on the hill,
And nought but the nightingale's song in the grove:
'Twas then, by the cave of the mountain afar,
A Hermit his song of the night thus began;
No more with himself, or with nature, at war,
He thought as a sage, while he felt as a man:

"Ah! why thus abandoned to darkness and woe?
"Why thus, lonely Philomel, flows thy sad strain?
"For spring shall return, and a lover bestow,
"And thy bosom no trace of misfortune retain. [128]
"Yet, if pity inspire thee, ah! cease not thy lay,
"Mourn, sweetest complainer! man calls thee to mourn:
"O sooth him, whose pleasures like thine pass away—
"Full quickly they pass—but they never return.

"Now gliding remote on the verge of the sky,
"The moon, half-extinguished, her crescent displays:
"But lately I marked, when majestic on high,
"She shone, and the planets were lost in her blaze.

"Roll on, thou fair orb, and with gladness pursue
"The path that conducts thee to splendour again:
"But man's faded glory no change shall renew —
"Ah fool! to exult in a glory so vain!

"Tis night, and the landscape is lovely no more:
"I mourn, but, ye woodlands, I mourn not for you;
"For morn is approaching, your charms to restore,
"Perfumed with fresh fragrance, and glittering with dew.
"Nor yet for the ravage of winter I mourn;
"Kind Nature the embryo blossom will save. —
"But when shall Spring visit the mouldering urn?
"O, when shall it dawn on the night of the grave? [129] "

'Twas thus, by the glare of false science betrayed,
That leads, to bewilder, and dazzles, to blind;
My thoughts wont to roam, from shade onward to shade,
Destruction before me, and sorrow behind.
"O pity, great Father of light," then I cried,
"Thy creature, who fain would not wander from Thee!
"Lo! humbled in dust, I relinquish my pride:
"From doubt and from darkness thou only canst free."

And darkness and doubt are now flying away:
No longer I roam in conjecture forlorn.
So breaks on the traveller, faint, and astray,
The bright and the balmy effulgence of morn.
See Truth, Love, and Mercy, in triumph descending,
And Nature all glowing in Eden's first bloom!
On the cold cheek of Death smiles and roses are blending,
And Beauty immortal awakes from the tomb!


## ODE TO PEACE. [130]

**WRITTEN IN THE YEAR 1756.**

I. 1.

Peace, heaven-descended maid! whose powerful voice
From antient darkness called the morn;
And hushed of jarring elements the noise,
When Chaos, from his old dominion torn,
With all his bellowing throng,
Far, far was hurled the void abyss along;
And all the bright angelic choir,
Striking, through all their ranks, the eternal lyre,
Poured, in loud symphony, the impetuous strain;
And every fiery orb and planet sung,
And wide, through Night's dark solitary reign,
Rebounding long and deep, the lays triumphant rung!
[131]


I. 2.

Oh, whither art thou fled, Saturnian Age!
Roll round again, majestic years!
To break the sceptre of tyrannic Rage;
From Woe's wan cheek to wipe the bitter tears;
Ye years, again roll round!
Hark! from afar what desolating sound,
While echoes load the sighing gales,
With dire presage the throbbing heart assails!
Murder, deep-roused, with all the whirlwind's haste,
And roar of tempest, from her cavern springs,
Her tangled serpents girds around her waist,
Smiles ghastly fierce, and shakes her gore-distilling wings.


I. 3.

The shouts, redoubling, rise
In thunder to the skies;
The nymphs, disordered, dart along,
Sweet powers of solitude and song,
Stunned with the horrors of discordant sound;

And all is listening, trembling round. [132]
Torrents, far heard amid the waste of night,
That oft have led the wanderer right,
Are silent at the noise.
The mighty Ocean's more majestic voice,
Drowned in superior din, is heard no more;
The surge in silence seems to sweep the foamy shore.


II. 1.

The bloody banner, streaming in the air,
Seen on yon sky-mixt mountain's brow,
The mingling multitudes, the madding car,
Driven in confusion to the plain below,
War's dreadful Lord proclaim.
Bursts out, by frequent fits, the expansive flame;
Snatched in tempestuous eddies, flies
The surging smoke o'er all the darkened skies;
The chearful face of heaven no more is seen;
The bloom of morning fades to deadly pale;
The bat flies transient o'er the dusky green,
And Night's foul birds along the sullen twilight sail.
[133]


II. 2.

Involved in fire-streaked gloom, the car comes on.
The rushing steeds grim Terror guides.
His forehead writhed to a relentless frown,
Aloft the angry Power of Battles rides.
Grasped in his mighty hand,
A mace, tremendous, desolates the land;
The tower rolls headlong down the steep,
The mountain shrinks before its wasteful sweep.
Chill horror the dissolving limbs invades,
Smit by the blasting lightning of his eyes;
A deeper gloom invests the howling shades;

Stripped is the shattered grove, and every verdure dies.


II. 3.

How startled Phrenzy stares,
Bristling her ragged hairs!
Revenge the gory fragment gnaws;
See, with her griping vulture claws
Imprinted deep, she rends the mangled wound!
Hate whirls her torch sulphureous round. [134]
The shrieks of agony, and clang of arms,
Re-echo to the hoarse alarms,
Her trump terrific blows.
Disparting from behind, the clouds disclose,
Of kingly gesture, a gigantic form,
That with his scourge sublime rules the careering storm.


III. 1.

Ambition, outside fair! within as foul
As fiends of fiercest heart below,
Who ride the hurricanes of fire, that roll
Their thundering vortex o'er the realms of woe,
Yon naked waste survey;
Where late was heard the flute's mellifluous lay;
Where late the rosy-bosomed hours,
In loose array, danced lightly o'er the flowers;
Where late the shepherd told his tender tale;
And, wakened by the murmuring breeze of morn,
The voice of chearful Labour filled the dale;
And dove-eyed Plenty smiled, and waved her liberal horn.
[135]


III. 2.

Yon ruins, sable from the wasting flame,
But mark the once resplendent dome;
The frequent corse obstructs the sullen stream,
And ghosts glare horrid from the sylvan gloom.
How sadly silent all!
Save where, outstretched beneath yon hanging wall,
Pale Famine moans with feeble breath,
And Anguish yells, and grinds his bloody teeth.
Though vain the Muse, and every melting lay,
To touch thy heart, unconscious of remorse!
Know, monster, know, thy hour is on the way;
I see, I see the years begin their mighty course.


III. 3.

What scenes of glory rise
Before my dazzled eyes!
Young zephyrs wave their wanton wings,
And melody celestial rings.
All blooming on the lawn the nymphs advance,
And touch the lute, and range the dance: [136]
And the blithe shepherds, on the mountain's side,
Arrayed in all their rural pride,
Exalt the festive note,
Inviting Echo from her inmost grot — —
But ah! the landscape glows with fainter light;
It darkens, swims, and flies for ever from my sight.


IV. 1.

Illusions vain! Can sacred Peace reside
Where sordid gold the breast alarms,
Where Cruelty inflames the eye of Pride,
And Grandeur wantons in soft Pleasure's arms?
Ambition, these are thine!
These from the soul erase the form divine;

And quench the animating fire,
That warms the bosom with sublime desire.
Thence the relentless heart forgets to feel,
And Hatred triumphs on the o'erwhelming brow,
And midnight Rancour grasps the cruel steel;
Blaze the blue flames of death, and sound the shrieks of woe.
[137]


IV. 2.

From Albion fled, thy once beloved retreat,
What regions brighten in thy smile,
Creative Peace! and underneath thy feet
See sudden flowers adorn the rugged soil?
In bleak Siberia blows,
Waked by thy genial breath, the balmy rose?
Waved over by thy magic wand,
Does life inform fell Lybia's burning sand?
Or does some isle thy parting flight detain,
Where roves the Indian through primæval shades;
Haunts the pure pleasures of the sylvan reign,
And, led by Reason's light, the path of Nature treads?


IV. 3.

On Cuba's utmost steep,
Far leaning o'er the deep,
The Goddess' pensive form was seen:
Her robe, of Nature's varied green,
Waved on the gale; grief dimmed her radiant eyes,
Her bosom heaved with boding sighs. [138]
She eyed the main; where, gaining on the view,
Emerging from the ethereal blue,
Midst the dread pomp of war,
Blazed the Iberian streamer from afar:
She saw; and, on refulgent pinions borne,

Slow winged her way sublime, and mingled with the morn.


# [139] THE

## TRIUMPH OF MELANCHOLY.

Memory, be still! why throng upon the thought
These scenes so deeply stained with sorrow's dye?
Is there in all thy stores no cheerful draught,
To brighten yet once more in Fancy's eye?


Yes—from afar a landscape seems to rise,
Embellished by the lavish hand of spring;
Thin gilded clouds float lightly through the skies,
And laughing loves disport on fluttering wing.


How blest the youth in yonder valley laid!
What smiles in every conscious feature play!
While, to the murmurs of the breezy glade,
His merry pipe attunes the rural lay. [140]


Hail, Innocence! whose bosom all serene,
Feels not, as yet, the internal tempest roll.
Oh, ne'er may care distract thy placid mein!
Ne'er may the shades of doubt o'erwhelm thy soul!


Vain wish! for lo, in gay attire concealed,
Yonder she comes! the heart-inflaming fiend!
(Will no kind power the helpless stripling shield!)
Swift to her destined prey see Passion bend!

O smile accurst, to hide the worst designs!
Now with blithe eye she wooes him to be blest;
While round her arm, unseen, a serpent twines — —
And lo, she hurls it hissing at his breast!


And, instant, lo, his dizzy eyeball swims
Ghastly, and reddening darts a frantic glare;
Pain, with strong grasp, distorts his writhing limbs,
And Fear's cold hand erects his frozen hair. [141]


Is this, O life, is this thy boasted prime!
And does thy spring no happier prospect yield!
Why should the sunbeam paint thy glittering clime,
When the keen mildew desolates the field!


How memory pains! Let some gay theme beguile
The musing mind, and sooth to soft delight.
Ye images of woe, no more recoil!
Be life's past scenes wrapt in oblivious night.


Now when fierce Winter, armed with wasteful power,
Heaves the wild deep that thunders from afar;
How sweet to sit in this sequestered bower,
To hear, and but to hear, the mingling war!


Ambition here displays no gilded toy,
That tempts on desperate wing the soul to rise;
Nor Pleasure's paths to wilds of woe decoy,
Nor Anguish lurks in Grandeur's proud disguise. [142]

Oft has Contentment cheered this lone abode,
With the mild languish of her smiling eye;
Here Health in rosy bloom has often glowed,
While loose-robed Quiet stood enamoured by.


Even the storm lulls to more profound repose;
The storm these humble walls assails in vain.
The shrub is sheltered, when the whirlwind blows,
While the oak's mighty ruin strows the plain.


Blow on, ye winds! Thine, Winter, be the skies;
And toss the infuriate surge, and vales lay waste.
Nature thy temporary rage defies;
To her relief the gentler Seasons haste.


Throned in her emerald car, see Spring appear!
(As Fancy wills, the landscape starts to view.)
Her emerald car the youthful Zephyrs bear,
Fanning her bosom with their pinions blue. [143]


Around the jocund Hours are fluttering seen,
And lo, her rod the rose-lip'd Power extends!
And lo, the lawns are decked in living green,
And Beauty's bright-eyed train from Heaven descends!


Haste, happy days, and make all Nature glad — —
But will all Nature joy at your return?
O, can ye cheer pale Sickness' gloomy bed,
Or dry the tears that bathe the untimely urn?


Will ye one transient ray of gladness dart,
Where groans the dungeon to the captive's wail?
To ease tired Disappointment's bleeding heart,

Will all your stores of softening balm avail!


When stern Oppression, in his harpy fangs,
From Want's weak grasp the last sad morsel bears,
Can ye allay the dying parent's pangs,
Whose infant craves relief with fruitless tears? [144]


For ah! thy reign, Oppression, is not past.
Who from the shivering limbs the vestment rends?
Who lays the once rejoicing village waste,
Bursting the ties of lovers and of friends!


But hope not, Muse, vain-glorious as thou art,
With the weak impulse of thy humble strain,
Hope not to soften Pride's obdurate heart,
When Errol's bright example shines in vain.


Then cease the theme. Turn, Fancy, turn thine eye,
Thy weeping eye, nor further urge thy flight.
Thy haunts, alas! no gleams of joy supply,
Or transient gleams, that flash and sink in night.


Yet fain the mind its anguish would forego:
Spread, then, Historic Muse, thy pictured scroll;
Bid the great scenes in all their splendour glow,
And rouse to thought sublime the exulting soul. [145]


What mingling pomps rush on the enraptured gaze!
Lo, where the gallant navy rides the deep!
Here, glittering towns their spiry turrets raise,
There, bulwarks overhang the shaggy steep.

Bristling with spears, and bright with burnished shields,
The embattled legions stretch their long array;
Discord's red torch, as fierce she scours the fields,
With bloody tincture stains the face of day.


And now the hosts in silence wait the sign.
Keen are their looks whom Liberty inspires!
Quick as the goddess darts along the line,
Each breast impatient burns with noble fires.


Her form how graceful! In her lofty mien
The smiles of love stern Wisdom's frown controul;
Her fearless eye, determined though serene,
Speaks the great purpose, and the unconquered soul. [146]


Mark, where Ambition leads the adverse band,
Each feature fierce and hagard, as with pain!
With menace loud he cries, while from his hand
He vainly strives to wipe the crimson stain.


Lo, at his call, impetuous as the storms,
Headlong to deeds of death the hosts are driven;
Hatred, to madness wrought, each face deforms,
Mounts the black whirlwind, and involves the heaven.


Now, Virtue, now thy powerful succour lend,
Shield them, for Liberty who dare to die — —
Ah, Liberty! will none thy cause befriend!
Are those thy sons, thy generous sons, that fly!


Not Virtue's self, when Heaven its aid denies,
Can brace the loosened nerves, or warm the heart;
Not Virtue's self can still the burst of sighs,

When festers in the soul misfortune's dart. [147]


See, where by terror and despair dismayed,
The scattering legions pour along the plain!
Ambition's car, in bloody spoils arrayed,
Hews its broad way, as Vengeance guides the rein.


But who is He, that, by yon lonely brook,
With woods o'erhung, and precipices rude,
Lies all abandoned, yet, with dauntless look,
Sees streaming from his breast the purple flood?


Ah, Brutus! ever thine be Virtue's tear!
Lo, his dim eyes to Liberty he turns,
As, scarce supported on her broken spear,
O'er her expiring son the goddess mourns.


Loose to the wind her azure mantle flies;
From her dishevelled locks she rends the plume;
No lustre lightens in her weeping eyes,
And on her tear-stained cheek no roses bloom. [148]


Meanwhile the world, Ambition, owns thy sway;
Fame's loudest trumpet labours with thy name;
For thee the Muse awakes her sweetest lay,
And Flattery bids for thee her altars flame.


Nor in life's lofty bustling sphere alone,
The sphere where monarchs and where heroes toil,
Sink Virtue's sons beneath Misfortune's frown,
While Guilt's thrilled bosom leaps at Pleasure's smile:

Full oft, where Solitude and Silence dwell,
Far, far remote, amid the lowly plain,
Resounds the voice of Woe from Virtue's cell:
Such is man's doom; and Pity weeps in vain.


Still grief recoils—How vainly have I strove,
Thy power, O Melancholy, to withstand!
Tired I submit; but yet, O yet remove,
Or ease the pressure of thy heavy hand. [149]


Yet, for a while, let the bewildered soul
Find in society relief from woe;
O yield, a while, to Friendship's soft controul;
Some respite, Friendship, wilt thou not bestow?


Come then, Philander! whose exalted mind
Looks down from far on all that charms the great;
For thou canst bear, unshaken and resigned,
The brightest smiles, the blackest frowns of Fate!


Come thou, whose love unlimited, sincere,
Nor faction cools, nor injury destroys;
Who lend'st to Misery's moan a pitying ear,
And feel'st with ecstasy another's joys:


Who know'st man's frailty, with a favouring eye
And melting heart, behold'st a brother's fall;
Who, unenslaved by Fashion's narrow tye,
With manly freedom follow'st Nature's call. [150]


And bring thy Delia, sweetly-smiling fair,
Whose spotless soul no rankling thoughts deform;
Her gentle accents calm each throbbing care,

And harmonize the thunder of the storm.


Though blest with wisdom, and with wit refined,
She courts no homage, nor desires to shine;
In her each sentiment sublime is joined
To female softness, and a form divine.


Come, and disperse the involving shadows drear;
Let chastened mirth the social hours employ.
O catch the swift-winged moment while 'tis near —
On swiftest wing the moment flies of joy.


Even while the careless disencumbered soul
Sinks, all dissolving, into pleasure's dream,
Even then to time's tremendous verge we roll,
With headlong haste, along life's surgey stream. [151]


Can gaiety the vanished years restore,
Or on the withering limbs fresh beauty shed,
Or soothe the sad INEVITABLE HOUR,
Or cheer the dark, dark mansions of the dead?


Still sounds the solemn knell, in Fancy's ear,
That called Eliza to the silent tomb;
With her how jocund rolled the sprightly year!
How shone the nymph in beauty's brightest bloom!


Ah! Beauty's bloom avails not in the grave!
Youth's lofty mien, nor Age's awful grace.
Moulder alike unknown the prince and slave,
Whelmed in the enormous wreck of human race.

The thought-fixed portraiture, the breathing bust,
The arch with proud memorials arrayed,
The long-lived pyramid shall sink in dust,
To dumb Oblivion's ever desert shade. [152]


Fancy from joy still wanders far astray.
Ah Melancholy, how I feel thy power!
Long have I laboured to elude thy sway —
But 'tis enough, for I resist no more.


The traveller thus, that o'er the midnight waste,
Through many a lonesome path is doomed to roam,
Wildered and weary sits him down at last;
For long the night, and distant far his home.


FINIS.

EDINBURGH:
Printed by James Ballantyne.